KM Lowe
TIDAL LOVE

TIDAL LOVE

*To Sara
Many thanks
KMLowe ♡*

KM LOWE

Author History

My name is **K**elly McMullen Lowe and I was born on March 19, 1986 to the proud parents of Christine Greenlees Beaumont Steedman and Hugh Patrick McMullen. My parents taught me the value of life and they showed me how to succeed. I married David Lowe, on December 30, 2006 and we have two wonderful children named Dylan and Tianna. Over the last couple of years, I was unwell, and I put all of my time into my family and reading. In 2012 I wanted to commit myself to writing my own novel. I have put a lot of time and effort into all of my books. I hope that you all enjoy them, as much I did writing them.

Acknowledgments

First of all, I would like to thank Francescca Wingfield for helping me to create a beautiful cover for my 21st novel. The moment I saw this cover, I just knew it suited this story.

Secondly, I would like to thank Karen Sanders for editing my book. This process is always so much easier with you on my side. I could not ask for anyone better to polish my manuscripts. You turn an ugly duckling into a beautiful swan. And you're such an amazing person.

Also, I would like to thank my family and friends for putting up with me over the last couple of years. My husband will get some sense out of me for a couple of weeks, until I start writing again. This book would not have been possible if it wasn't for the support of my husband. I love you to the moon and back.

Next, I would like to thank my children for being my little angels. I love you dearly and you mean the world to me. I hope that one day you will be able to read mummy's work. In the meantime, Dylan, you can read the blurb. My son is my little book worm. I hope when he gets older, he will still enjoy reading just as much.

Finally, to all the ladies in my street team and review group, I can't thank you enough for sticking by me lately. I love you all. I can't possibly mention you all, because I would be sure to forget someone, and each of you mean so much to me.

Special Acknowledgements

I would like to thank Yvonne Eason for everything she does for me, from kicking my butt when I need it, plaguing my life for more books, and for beta reading my work. I love you, lady. I probably would have given up lately, but you have kept me going. For that, I thank you from the bottom of my heart.

Much Love,

Kelly

xx

Dedications

This book is dedicated to my sprinting buddy, Toya Richardson. Without her sprinting with me, I probably wouldn't have been anywhere near publishing this book. This was my lockdown project. I wasn't fussed about finishing it, but once I started it, the characters captured my heart and it became very easy to write their story.

So, thank you, Toya. Your friendship, love, and support mean so much to me. I can't wait to see you again in 2022.

Much love,

Kelly

XXX

Prologue

Harleigh

How on Earth did my life become so messed up? I had it all; the house, the fiancé, the great job... now, I have nothing.

Well, I still have the fiancé, more's the pity. My life has become non-existent because of his obsessive ways.

I was an English teacher, teaching eleven to eighteen-year-olds in a secondary school in Glasgow. I used to make the fifty-minute commute there every day from Stirling. It was something I loved. I woke up happy every morning, knowing I was doing something I wanted to do. Then, along come Martin. He was a real estate developer. All was great in the beginning, but I think the power from him becoming a partner in his company went straight to his head, because life changed.

Now, I must work from home as a freelance editor because it's the only thing I can do to bring in an income. I can't leave the house without him. The few times I have nipped out on my own, it caused World War Three, and I ended up with serious injuries. I can't even speak to my friends without him around, so now I don't bother seeing anyone because he just growls at everyone, and it's uncomfortable for them and me. I'm living like a recluse.

My family is concerned about me, but what do I say? "Oh, yeah. You have every right to be worried about me. My fiancé is beating me to a pulp when nothing goes his way, and he despises the ground you all walk on." That would make for an interesting conversation, one where my older brother, Gavin, would end up in prison because he would kill Martin with his bare hands and enjoy inflicting pain on him for everything he did to me. It isn't worth thinking about.

I look at the clock and notice it's nearly time for Martin to return home. My heart feels like it misses a beat. The butterflies swarm in my stomach, and they're not the good kind. They're the kind that appear when danger is near.

I try to steady my nerves. I've got everything prepared. His dinner's in the oven, the housework is done, and I'm dressed in something my grandmother would wear. I hate the way I have to dress. Anything I used to wear annoys him. I'm a slut, a whore, someone asking for trouble. And nothing I ever wore was provocative. I dressed casually most of the time. I was a schoolteacher, and I dressed impeccably to make a good impression on my students. I didn't like to show a lot of skin back then, but now, I'm as well wearing a snowsuit all year long. The only time my skin is free to breathe is when I take a shower. Even then, it's a quick shower so I don't waste water, which will cause more arguments and possibly more bruises to add to my collection.

It's safe to say that my life is an existence. One I'm getting so tired of. I feel older than my years here, and I fear if I don't do something to get away, I'll end up dead.

I save the document on my computer and close it. Martin doesn't like me working on anything when he's home, but he can ignore me and work through whatever he likes. He's a hypocrite. One I've come to loathe. One I've tried every way to get away from, apart from bringing in my family, because I don't want them to get hurt. I don't want them to suffer because of my choices. I need to work through this mess myself. I made my bed. I've inflicted this on myself for being weak. I can sort my life out myself.

I *will* sort this out myself.

The front door slams shut, and I jump. I quickly stand from the table and make myself busy at the oven. I take out Martin's dinner and place it down on the table just as he walks into the kitchen. He walks over to me and grips my chin in his hands. I look into his navy eyes and cringe when I see the deep, dark menace I've come to know. He looks pissed off, but that's nothing unusual lately. He's constantly pissed off. The man I once liked is long gone.

"H-hi," I stammer.

I hate how he makes me feel weak and out of control. I was a strong, independent person before he changed me into this quivering wreck. Now, I'm a shadow of the person I once was. I don't like the person I am now, and I can't see me ever being the same again… not as long as I live here under his wrath.

"You look…" He looks me up and down and laughs before he turns his back on me. "Ridiculous."

The blood runs cold through my veins and I look down at my feet. I hope and pray the ground opens up and swallows me whole. Sometimes the mental abuse is worse than the physical abuse. I can cover up the scars and forget about them, but the words he uses are on repeat all the damn time. It's like he takes pleasure in dragging me down.

"What is this?" He pushes the plate slightly in my direction.

"A chicken chasseur."

All of a sudden, without any warning, the plate speeds through the air and just misses my head before smashing off the cupboards behind me. I shriek. I'm angry that I cooked that meal all day, but I'm terrified of the mood he's in.

I can't take this anymore. I look at Martin, who has the biggest smirk on his face. He looks evil and deranged. I've spent all day cooking and cleaning, for what? For him to come home and have a tantrum.

"What the fuck is your problem!" I straighten my spine and grow a backbone. I need to take back some control of my life. I'm fed up of being treated like a piece of dirt. I've let it go on long enough.

This ends tonight. I either walk away from this house and never return, or my family gets me back in a wooden box. Either way, it ends. It has to.

"Really? Tonight is not the night for you to be dramatic, Harleigh." He stands from the table and marches over to me, gripping my throat tightly. "You belong to me and you will do as I fucking say. I don't work all hours of the day to eat chicken."

His grip tightens on my throat and I feel my eyes bulging out of my head. He pushes me out of his hands, laughs hysterically, and walks out of the kitchen. I know what I'd like to feed the bastard. Rat poison.

I rub at my neck, hoping to help the air flow to and from my lungs more easily. When I can breathe more freely, I stumble forward and grab Martin's car key from the worktop. I see the path from the kitchen to the front door and I take a few steps to test the waters. I don't want to run and draw attention to myself, but I can't take baby steps either. I need to get out of here, and preferably unnoticed by the monster I thought I once loved. I shake my head at that thought, because I must have been crazy to get into this relationship.

Nothing comes to stop me, so I take one step, two steps, three steps... until I finally reach the front door. I sigh with relief and turn the door handle slowly. Only, when it's all the way down and I try to open it, it doesn't budge. I feel my smile disintegrate when realisation hits me. Of course, he was never going to make things easy for me. He was never going to let me walk out of here.

"Tut, tut, tut..."

I look over my shoulder and Martin's dangling the house keys on his finger. I feel my heart pound in my chest. I know he isn't going to let my disobedience go unnoticed. I'm going to pay for trying to break out of this cage.

"Please, Martin, just let me go. I can't do this anymore. *We* can't do this anymore. This relationship is killing us. It's toxic." I sob erratically.

"There is no *we* in this house, Harleigh. You're nothing. Do you hear me? Nothing!" he yells. "You're just the pathetic dogsbody."

He stomps closer to me and pushes me against the door. He rips my shirt open, sending the buttons flying everywhere. He's done this before, but I won't let him take another strip from me.

I knee him in the groin, and he steps back from me enough to let me run away from him. I aim for the stairs, but he catches my leg and I fall up the steps, hitting my head on the step in front of me. My head feels fuzzy and my vision swims in and out of focus. I try to stand up and run, but Martin rounds on me from behind and pushes me into the stairs. Trying to break free from him, my face burns from the friction the carpet is causing. I feel like my back is going to snap with the pressure he has on me. The need to get Martin off me is heavy, but his weight is even heavier. I have no chance of getting him off me, not with how fuzzy my head feels and the nausea floating around my stomach.

I'm defeated before it's even begun.

"You. Will. Not. Leave. Me. Bitch." He spits into my neck.

He grabs the back of my neck with one hand and holds me down like someone would with a wild animal. His spare hand rips my trousers and pants down to my knees. It's at this moment that I give in fighting this. The power is being drained from me by the second. He's going to win. He always wins.

"This is mine." He grabs my crotch and rams his finger inside of me painfully. It's like he gets off on hurting me.

The tears fall down my cheeks relentlessly and my mind drifts off to another world where fluffy unicorns and glitter is the worst that can happen.

I like my make believe world.

Life would be so much better in my other world, away from all that's evil. Away from this man.

Chapter 1

One Year Later

Harleigh

Looking out into the schoolyard where children play, it's always a happy place. Children are carefree and joyful. It's a time I can remember easily. Growing up, I wanted for nothing. I had everything I needed, including the love of my family and friends. I was one of those kids who looked forward to becoming an adult, living independently, but life changed quickly when reality hit me square in the face… literally. That first night when Martin come home from the pub with his colleagues and burst my lip should have been a wake-up call for me, but I forgave him time and time again.

"I'm sorry, Harleigh. I don't know what came over me. It was a terrible mistake that won't happen again. I promise. Please, forgive me."

"Miss Harrison?" I look over my shoulder to the open door towards one of my students. Thankfully, my memory was broken before I could get stuck too deep.

"Yes, Sharlene. What can I do for you?"

I clasp my shaky hands between my knees to hide my uneasiness.

"Do you have that extra work you said you'd have for me today?"

"Ah, yes, of course."

I remove my real-life mask and put in place my teacher mask, where I hide everything for my students' sake. What am I saying? I hide away from myself too, because at school, I'm just their teacher. I don't have to be anyone else. My students don't expect anything from me other than the person they've come to know and like. The person that teaches them everything they need to know about English.

I stand from my desk and open my bag. I take out the folder I put together for Sharlene to work on while she's away visiting family. The poor girl lost her mum three months ago and I've made sure to do all I can to help her study for her GCSEs next month. No child should have to bury a parent, especially not at a crucial stage of their learning, but cancer doesn't care whose door it knocks upon.

"Here we go. I've written down my email address on the front page in case you want to ask me anything when you're away."

"Thanks, Miss. I appreciate all you've done for me. You've made me realise that English is the route I want to take when I leave school."

I feel the pride soaring through me. If I never do anything right in my life again, Sharlene's words will echo in my head forever.

"I'm glad I could help you. Don't hesitate to contact me if you need anything. Anything at all."

"Thank you. See you in two weeks."

"Enjoy your trip."

I watch Sharlene's back, and for the first time in months, I have a genuine smile on my face. Returning to work after Martin's attack on me was hard, but it was something I needed to do to take back some control of my life. The headmaster of the school I used to work in was happy to have me back when I made the call. I commute daily and enjoy it. It's amazing what a bit of freedom does for the soul.

Each day, I take a piece of me back, but I doubt I'll ever be whole again. Too much pain and heartache were caused at the hands of someone who was supposed to love me.

"Miss Harrison, there is a visitor for you in reception," the receptionist says over the speaker.

I head out of my classroom and make my way along to the office. I have no idea who could be here for me, but it's only my family who know where I work.

I reach reception and see my brother, Gavin, leaning against the doorframe. He looks up as I approach.

"Thank you, Mrs Digby." I acknowledge the receptionist kindly.

"Whatever has got that smile back on your face, you need to bottle it up and save it," says Gavin, as I walk into his embrace and hug him tightly.

"I'm doing what I love again." I smile brightly. "Sign in and come along while I pack up my things." I motion for him to follow me to my classroom. "What are you doing here, Gav?"

"I just landed about an hour ago and I had to come and see my favourite sister. It's like Fort Knox to get in here."

"Your only sister." I laugh. "And it's all security measures now. It keeps us and the kids safe."

Gavin is a pilot and he spends much of his time in the air flying from country to country.

"How are you doing, honey?"

I shrug and sit back down at my desk. "I'm okay. I'm much better." I try to hide behind the lie I keep telling myself. Maybe one day I'll believe it too.

Gavin sits on a pupil's desk in front of me and leans his elbows on his knees.

"We're all concerned about you, Harl."

"You needn't be. I'm good. I'm working. Surviving," I sigh, frustrated. "I'm much better than I was."

"But you're not living, doll."

"What do you want me to do, huh?" I snap.

It's the same argument every time I see my family. I think they expect me to be jumping through hoops, swinging from trees, and partying on a school night. None of which was ever me.

"I just don't want to see you fading away to nothing. What is it? Five weeks until the summer holidays? Let me pay for a trip. Get out of here. Explore the world. Find yourself again. You deserve it."

I watch my brother with bated breath. I know he's only doing what he thinks is best, but I'm more than capable of living my life the way I want to. I don't need everyone telling me what to do, even though a holiday sounds good.

"Where would I go? I'm barely living here, as you've just told me. I'm not sure I could go on holiday alone."

My house has become my safe haven. I can't imagine being anywhere else alone.

"Let me book somewhere for you. A surprise."

I close my eyes and think about taking a trip. Some sun, sea, and cocktails. No reminders of everything I've been through. No work. Just time for me to live a while.

"Eurgh!" I growl out my response. "Do I have much of a choice?"

Gavin shakes his head. "Nope. I'm not trying to control you or be bossy, I just want to see you happy again, doll. I want my carefree sister back."

I take in a deep breath and let it out slowly. I don't want to break his heart and tell him that person could be gone forever.

Gavin has always been able to get me to say yes to anything. That's probably why he got the short straw and is gracing my classroom with his presence.

"Okay." I sigh. "Just nowhere over the top."

His smile lights up the room. "I promise. You'll love it."

Gavin jumps off the table and leans over to kiss my cheek. He looks like one of my excited pupils after lunch.

"I love you, Harleigh. I just want to see my happy, vibrant sister again. I hate seeing the pain in your eyes."

"I know. I love you, too."

Gavin winks at me and leaves my classroom behind. He's always been the best big brother ever. Even when he's being a pain in my backside, which is regularly.

I just can't bear to see the hurt and pain I'm causing my family. Maybe a holiday will do us all good.

Chapter 2

Six weeks later

Harleigh

My cases are packed, my passport is in my bag, and I'm ready to see where my brother has booked for me. I'm determined not to let any memories or voices in my head spoil this holiday. I'm going away… alone. I *can* do this. I *will* do this.

Gavin, my parents, and my other brother, Sebastian, are all hovering around my kitchen. I approach them slowly, plastering a smile on my face; something I'm getting really good at. I had to be a good actress when I lived with Martin. It's just hard to break old habits, because I'm aware my family can see through my act. They know I'm still hurting from my time with him, and nothing they do or say will change that. I need to move at my own pace, and I realise it isn't fast enough for my family.

"There's my girl." My dad stands up from his stool and takes me into his arms. "All packed?"

"I sure am. Who's going to put me out of my misery and tell me where I'm going?" I pull back from my dad. "I can't believe I've let you talk me into this."

"It will do you the world of good, sweetheart." Dad pats my cheek.

"I believe I'm the one to tell you where you're off to, baby sis." Gavin walks towards me with an envelope outstretched. "Four weeks, all paid for, private transportation is waiting at the airport to take you to your hotel."

"Four weeks. I said a break, Gavin. Jesus Christ." I chastise my brother and shake my head.

The nerves are picking up; my palms are sweaty, my heart is racing, and my vision is blurred. All classic signs of a panic attack. All signs that I'm so used to.

A few deep breaths and I try to calm myself down. *I will not break. I will not break. I will not break.*

"You'll love it, sis." Seb wraps his arms around my shoulders and kisses my head. "Tell her where she's going, Gav."

"You'll be flying into Bourgas Airport, where you'll be taken to your hotel in Old Nessebar. I've organised transport so you don't need to worry about a thing."

I look at my brother like he just spoke in another language. That airport and place rings no bells to me.

"Bulgaria. You're going to Bulgaria, Harl. It's a good mix of culture and nightlife," says Gavin. "I thought it would be perfect for you, especially Old Nessebar."

I want to groan and protest. Bulgaria has never been high on my list of places to visit. In fact, it wasn't on my list at all. I know absolutely nothing about Bulgaria. At least if it was Spain or France, I'd have a little knowledge of the language and culture. But, oh no, my brother must go completely over the top.

"I've been there several times." Gavin tilts his head and lifts my chin. "Old Nessebar is the most beautiful village ever. You'll thank me when you come home."

I roll my eyes. I don't know whether to laugh or cry. None of this impromptu holiday thing is me. I need a break, I know I do, but flying to God knows where, alone, is maybe a little step too far for me.

"I'll be the judge of that." I pull the envelope out of his hand and put it into my hand luggage.

"This is some Bulgarian lev to tide you over for a few days." Seb hands me another envelope.

I open the envelope and gasp. "A few days."

"It's just a little something from all of us, sweetheart. We want you to go and have some fun," says my dad.

I know I've put my family through hell lately, and I don't want to see that look of pity anymore, but I don't want them to mollycoddle me either. Maybe this trip will be the making of me. They can live their lives for a few weeks without worrying about me, and I can get away from here without looking over my shoulder, wondering which one is going to stage an intervention next.

"Okay then. Let's get this holiday started," I state, more for my family than myself.

All I can do now is go away for four weeks and try to enjoy this break away from reality. Maybe some sun, sea, and whatever they drink in Bulgaria will be the making of me.

School's out for summer.

Chapter 3

Harleigh

The moment I step out of the aeroplane; the heat hits me in the face. I take a few moments to relish that feeling. It's like that little bit of sun melts a small amount of ice from around my heart and I feel like I can breathe easier. The freedom to do whatever I want is like winning a million pounds.

I was a kind, caring person before Martin got his claws into me, but now, I feel like I'll never trust and enjoy the company of another man again. If I'm out with my family for a meal, I look down at my hands and feet all the time, because I hate making eye contact with strangers. I hate that I feel so weak and small. I hate the insecurities that follow me around now.

Walking through the airport, claiming my baggage, and then finally finding my driver holding my name plaque, it was all done in a bit of a blur. I was nervous and excited about being here alone, but now I want to explore and see what Bulgaria has to offer. I want to hide in my own little bubble while I'm here and just enjoy my time without trying to please everyone around me. This is very much out of my comfort zone, but I can be anything I want while I'm here, because no one knows me, and no one knows what I've been through. I can swim, walk, sunbathe, and read as many books as I can. I have four weeks of me time, something I've not had a lot of lately. Well, I had a lot of time alone when I was with Martin, but I wasn't allowed to do anything I liked.

"You visit here before, Miss?" asks Frank, my driver, breaking through the thoughts running through my head.

I shake my head, looking out at the magnificent views over the sea.

"No. My brother thought I'd love it here." I roll my eyes under my sunglasses, because as much as I want to disagree with Gavin, I know I'll really enjoy staying here. It has a nice feel to it already.

"Nessebar is a fantastic place. And The Ranch is the best hotel to stay in." He speaks in broken English, but I can understand him well.

"Is it a new hotel?"

"New owner. Refurbished. Beautiful." He kisses his fingers and makes me smile.

Frank manoeuvres us along the waterfront up a hill. The old buildings are magnificent. It reminds me of an old western style village. My heart rate picks up again, but this time, not because of any impending panic attacks.

"Here we are." Frank turns off the car and gets out to help me.

I don't know how much my brother paid for Frank's services, but he has treated me like a queen since he picked me up thirty minutes ago. It certainly beats the coach transfer I'm used to taking on holiday.

I step out onto the cobbled street and look up to the hotel I'm staying in. Again, it's a beautiful old building. It takes my breath away. It's indescribable.

"Have a good trip, Miss."

"Thank you, Frank." I reach into my purse and hand him over a twenty lev note. I read in the tour guide that Gavin had inside the envelope with my tickets that Bulgarians live from their tips. I'll take great pleasure in tipping people like Frank.

"No need. Your brother did all the tipping necessary."

I take his hand and close his fingers around the note. "I am not my brother. Thank you for all your help, Frank."

"My pleasure, Miss Harleigh."

I walk into the hotel and head straight over to the receptionist. It seems like a calm hotel. Everything is still and beautiful. The perfect getaway for me to rest and relax.

"Hello. I have a room booked. My name is Harleigh Harrison."

"Yes. Welcome, Mrs Harrison."

"Miss. It's Miss Harrison," I correct the young woman.

"I'm sorry. I shouldn't assume everyone is married when they come here. I apologise."

I shake my head. "An honest mistake. Please, don't worry about it. I'm looking forward to exploring everything there is on offer here."

"I hope you enjoy your stay. If I can get you anything, or assist with anything, please, just ask. You're in room 12. Oliver here will help you to your room. There is a welcome pack in your room. It will tell you everything you need to know about the hotel."

"Thank you." I take my key card and turn to walk away when I bang into a solid, muscular chest. "I'm so sorry. I didn't..."

I bend down to pick up my key card at the same time as the man I just walked into.

"Here we go. No harm done," comes a charming Scottish accent.

I take my key card from him and smile. "Thank you. I'm not having the greatest start to this trip. I seem to have acquired a clumsy tendency."

"Well, we can't be having that now. What part of Scotland are you joining us from?"

"Stirling. Central belt."

"I know it well. Welcome to The Ranch. Manuela, can you please have a bottle of prosecco taken up to the lady's room?"

"Oh, I couldn't possibly accept your generous offer."

I finally look at the man in front of me instead of diverting my eyes anywhere other than at him. The man in front of me is an Adonis. His short-ish brown hair is messed up stylishly. His dark brown eyes are sparkling at me. His lightly tanned skin just sets off the whole package.

"Please, I insist. It's on management."

"Oh..." I look down at the man's dress shorts and open white shirt. He doesn't scream management, but I've made a big enough fool of myself. "Well, thank you..." I pause because we haven't exchanged names.

"You're welcome. And the name is Giovani."

"Thank you, Giovani. My name is Harleigh."

"Beautiful name for a beautiful lady."

I feel the heat rise through my cheeks and I look down at the key card in my hand. It's only now that I realise Oliver is waiting to escort me to my room.

"I should be going."

I point over my shoulder and scurry off like a little lost mouse. Taking compliments has never been a strong point for me, but since my ex, I struggle to hear anything nice about myself.

Oliver pushes the button for the lift, and moments later, we walk inside. I dare to look out into the reception area and Giovani is smiling brightly at me. His smile would brighten up the darkest of storms. I've never been so affected by a man before. My heart is racing, my skin prickles, and my head is spinning. This is ludicrous. I just said not too long ago that I'd never look at another man again.

Why the hell am I acting like a lovesick puppy?

Get a grip, Harleigh.

Chapter 4

Giovani

"Boss..." Manuela breaks through the haze.

"Yes?" I clear my throat.

"Prosecco. Any particular kind?"

I smile at Harleigh through the closing lift doors. Her beautiful long light brown hair is cascading down around her shoulders in ringlets. She's a beauty.

"Just the best. Nothing but the best for Miss..."

"Miss Harrison, boss."

Miss Harrison.

"As you were. I'll be in my office for a little while." I walk away from the check-in desk feeling like I'm floating on a cloud.

No woman has ever turned my head like Harleigh. I can see something in her, but I don't know what it is. She's bright and quiet, just like my hotel. Its tranquillity is its best asset. There's a story behind the walls, but on the outside, it's masked by beauty.

Life has never been dull for me, but visiting Nessebar made my life complete. It made me the person I am today. It made me forget about the pain and embarrassment of a broken relationship. It healed me piece by piece and made me realise that life is for living. Who couldn't live in this beautiful country and be happy?

"You fancy a night out tonight, bro?" asks Lucca, my younger brother, who is visiting from Scotland. I say visiting, but he's a permanent fixture lately.

"Sure. What do you have in mind?"

"What about a trip over to Sunny Beach, or just a few drinks around here? I need to let off some steam."

"I don't fancy Sunny Beach tonight, but I'm up for a few drinks around here. What's up?"

"Dad."

I roll my eyes at that one word. Lucca and our father have a love/hate relationship. Since our parents moved back to Italy three years ago, they expected Lucca to go back with them. But he's young, independent, and looking to see the world. He isn't a child anymore, and I don't blame him. I can't imagine being tied to the one place. I like my freedom too much.

"Dad only wants what's best for you."

"And Italy isn't that. Maybe one day I'll settle down there, but not now."

"Okay then. Do you want to have dinner here before we hit the bars?"

I need to change the subject, because I won't have Lucas on a downward spiral. It has taken me months to get him to where he is now. He walked out of his life in Glasgow and showed up on my doorstep one morning at four a.m. We got drunk and put the world to rights. The rest, as they say, is history.

"Sure. I'll meet you in the restaurant at eight and we can decide what to do. Are you okay? You looked far away when you entered the office."

"I'm good. Just busy. Lots of new arrivals today and tomorrow."

Which is only half of the truth. I can't be dealing with being taunted by my brother, now or ever. He will mean well, but he will only drive me up the wall. My family know my history and they've all been on my case about settling down, but after everything I faced at the hands of a woman, I'm lucky to be standing here today with everything I have. I vowed after that living nightmare, I would never let a woman get her claws stuck into me again… ever.

That's why I made this life here. I love my job. I love my life. I'm never going back to the dark place I once was.

Chapter 5

Harleigh

When I arrived at my room this afternoon, I contemplated whether to hide away or face the world. Instead of doing the only thing I know how to do – hide – I did the next best thing. I grabbed a book from my hand luggage, changed into lighter clothes, threw a beach bag over my shoulder, and exited my hotel room with my head held high, or as high as my timid self would allow. My sunglasses give me a little safety net as I hide behind them, and I feel more confident than I have in such a long time.

"Miss Harrison…" I look over my shoulder to see Manuela walking towards me. "Shall I ask Oliver to place your bottle of prosecco in your fridge?"

"Oh, please, don't worry about it." I stutter over my words.

You wouldn't think I was an English teacher with the way I've been speaking since I touched down in Bulgaria. I feel like I'm learning to talk to people all over again.

"Miss, our boss won't be happy if I tell him I didn't deliver your bottle, compliments of the management."

"Okay." I smile warmly. "The fridge will be grand."

"Enjoy your day, Miss Harrison."

"Thank you. You too, Manuela."

I walk out of the hotel and take in a deep breath. I look around myself for the first time and I'm in the middle of a square. I don't know why I didn't notice before, but the area is bustling with tourists. The small play park across the road has children of all ages playing, laughing, yelling in many different languages, and having fun. There is nothing more satisfying than seeing children enjoy life. It's one thing I love about teaching.

Walking closer to the park, I notice a restaurant/bar that looks out over the sea, set upon a cliff. It looks beautiful and peaceful. The front of house guy waves to me, and I smile brightly at him.

"Hello. Would you like to come inside?"

I nod. "I would. Thank you."

He shows me to a table overlooking the sea. I'm glad he picked this table, because it's gorgeous. It's like he read my mind. It wasn't the delicious smell of food drawing me in here, it was the sight of the glorious, calm Black Sea.

"A beautiful table for a beautiful lady."

I blush.

"Thank you."

It looks like I need to get used to accepting compliments here. Everyone is very friendly and approachable. I've probably received more compliments since arriving in Bulgaria than I have in the last year back at home.

"What would m'lady like to drink?"

"Oh." I look behind him at the stocked bar. "Do you have pink gin?"

"Absolutely."

"I'll have a pink gin and lemonade, thank you."

"Coming right up."

I give the sea my full attention. The black waves crashing against the rocks below me is calming for the soul. It's no wonder everyone here is happy. The sun is shining brightly, the atmosphere is euphoric, and the whole place is beautiful.

My phone ringing distracts me, and I see Gavin's name flashing on the screen. I wondered when he would check in. I'm surprised it took him so long, especially since I touched down a couple of hours ago.

"Hello, Gavin."

"Hey. You arrived then."

"Of course. Don't sound so shocked. My driver was very attentive and dropped me off at the doorstep of my hotel."

"And?"

"And…" I look out over the sea again and sigh contentedly. "It's beautiful. I've just called into a lovely little bar/restaurant across from the hotel. I only came in for a drink, but I might even eat dinner here in a little while. It smells delicious."

"If you find the right restaurants, you'll want to eat all day long."

"Any recommendations?"

"Let me have a think and I'll send you some details. I hope you have a great trip, Harls. You deserve it."

"Thank you, Gav."

"Well, don't be a stranger. I want to see and hear all about your trip."

"You'll be the first to hear about it. I must go just now. Take care."

I cut off the phone call and turn my phone onto silent. I'll never get to explore and have fun if my family are going to check up on me every minute of the day. I love them dearly, but this is an escape from reality. I want to live each moment while I can. I won't be able to do that if I spend all of my time answering phone calls to my family back home.

***

"Harleigh, isn't it?" a voice breaks through my thoughts as I read my book.

I look up and see Giovani and another man being seated at the table to my side. I look down at my watch and it reads eight p.m. I've been sitting here for about three hours. To my horror, the restaurant has filled up since I was last aware of my surroundings. Couples, families, and groups of friends have all joined various tables. It's no longer that calm place I entered. I was transported to another world by the talented Tillie Marie. Her books have a habit of drawing me in, breaking my heart, and then healing me piece by glorious piece.

"Hello. I'm sorry. I was a million miles away."

"Easy enough to do here. How was your food?" Giovani gestures to my near empty plate.

"It was lovely. The best pasta dish I've had in a long time."

"Are you going to introduce me?" asks the gentleman sitting opposite Giovani.

"Sorry. Lucca this is Harleigh. Harleigh, this is my annoying little brother, Lucca."

"Nice to meet you." Lucca reaches over and holds his hand out to me.

"Likewise."

His large hand encases mine in his and I feel a sudden wave of anxiety flow through me from head to toe, but I try to take in a deep breath without being too obvious. I hate touching people full stop, but strangers always make me extra cautious.

I really need to get this blushing under control. It makes me look so immature and I hate it. I'm a grown adult, for goodness' sake.

Do I continue talking to them, say goodbye and go, or sit here and read my book?

I don't want to interrupt their dinner, so I immerse myself back into my book, all the while drinking my gin. I'm not sure I can concentrate on my book now, because all I can think about is the man sitting at the table beside me. I can hear his Scottish accent and it does something to me. Maybe it's because I haven't heard my own native accent since I left Glasgow this morning. Maybe it's just that man. Maybe it's a thousand other reasons that I can't even comprehend while sitting here.

"Excuse me." I look over at Giovani and his brother. "If I'm being a little forward, just tell me, but I know you're traveling alone. I was wondering if you'd care to join us for a few drinks. My brother here is an expert on the best bars in Bulgaria. I believe he's worked hard on getting that reputation." Giovani shrugs at Lucca, rolling his eyes.

"We can't all be old coffin dodgers now, can we?" Lucca ribs him back.

I feel a smile creep over my face. The brothers are doing something many people have tried and failed to do over the last twelve months: make me laugh.

"I couldn't possibly impose on your plans, and I'm afraid I'd be no company. I plan on going back to my room and catching up on some sleep after a long day."

Just saying that out loud makes me sound so dull. I'm trying to improve my life, not go backwards. This holiday is supposed to be the making of me.

"Sleep's for old people," Lucca says, taking a big gulp of his beer.

"Ignore him." Giovani throws a napkin at his brother and I laugh. The simple sound is alien to my own ears. "And you wouldn't be imposing. I wouldn't have asked if I didn't want you to join us."

I sit in silence for a few moments. It was like I was hoping someone would make the decision for me. I've grown so accustomed to not being able to make my own choices, that when I can make a choice for myself, it feels weird and uncomfortable. And just like that, I find myself transported right back to the past. A place I don't want to go again.

I won't go there, not right now.

"Besides, you'll be doing me a huge favour sharing the babysitting duties." Giovani points over to his brother, who is making faces.

Lucca splutters on his beer at his own childish behaviour and I laugh at him.

"I'm not exactly dressed to go out," I look down at my summer casual attire and cringe.

"You're in Bulgaria. There is no right or wrong way to dress. But, to put your mind at rest, you look beautiful just the way you are."

"Okay," I say, much to my shock and horror. "If you're sure you don't mind me tagging along."

If I'm being honest, I probably wouldn't frequent bars on my own, so this gives me a taste of what Bulgarian nightlife has to offer.

"Of course we don't mind."

I nod at Giovani and lift my bag to put my book away and pay for my meal.

I flag down the waiter and ask for my bill. He must understand me, because he nods and walks away from my table. It's a different waiter to when I arrived earlier and I'm sad about that because I'd like to give him a nice tip for being so helpful.

The few moments it takes for him to come back make me nervous. I try to find any excuse to get out of this bar crawl with the guys. They seem genuine enough, and one of them runs the hotel I'm staying in. I'm sure he's just being friendly. He's probably just afraid that I'll get lost on my own.

The waiter places down the tray with my bill.

"Thank you." I take out forty lev and place it in the little folder. I wave him off when he tries to give me change.

"Have a good evening." He nods at me with a warm smile.

I stand from my chair when Giovani and his brother stand. I don't quite know what to do now. I have never felt as awkward in my life. Do I follow them? Do I walk alongside them? Do I talk to them about pointless things? Eurgh! I'm one of the most socially awkward people to walk this planet. I should be ashamed of myself for feeling like this. I should be bright and bubbly like my family. Only, I'm apprehensive of everything, thinking everything is about to eat me. I'm fed up being skittish and nervous around people.

"So, what brings you to Bulgaria, Harleigh?" asks Lucca.

I shrug, wondering if I should tell them the truth. What the hell.

"My family railroaded me into being here. They thought I needed a break away from reality. My brother is a pilot and has travelled all over the world. He booked this holiday for me. So, here I am. I had no idea where I was going until this morning." I smile as we walk slowly down the cobbled street.

"You sound like you have an annoying brother just like me," Lucca jokes and nudges Giovani in the ribs.

"First drinks are on you for being cheeky. Annoying brothers wouldn't let you live with them for, how long has it been?" Giovani holds his hand over his ear, pretending he can't hear what Lucca is about to say.

"Yeah, yeah. Keep your knickers on. Come on, we can't not show your guest what Betty Lou has to offer. Her cocktails are divine, and she has happy hour. Buy one, get one free, all day every day."

"Oh, wow. I love cocktails, but they tend to not like me." I laugh.

And that's how our night started. We hit the cocktails, laughed, enjoyed each other's company, and got a bit tipsy.

***

Lucca got up to sing a song on the karaoke. By this point in the night, I fear I've had one too many cocktails and I would get up to sing on the karaoke and probably dance on the tables, and that is bad. I'm tone deaf. I can't string a tune together if my life depends on it. I like music, my voice just isn't on board. A cat's choir springs to mind.

"Are you having a good night?" Giovani sits back down beside me after his bathroom visit. He doesn't look any different than he did a few hours ago. Either he can hold his alcohol better than me and Lucca, or he's not drinking half as much as us.

"I am. I'm glad I came out with you guys now. Your brother is a hoot." I giggle at him singing *Achy Breaky Heart*. He sounds good to my ears, but I'm not sure if he actually is good, or if it's all down to the alcohol.

"That's one word for him." Giovani shakes his head and laughs. "I could think of many other words to describe him, they're just not as kind as yours."

Tonight has been a good night. It's been good to enjoy someone else's presence. I've got so used to my own company lately. I was too scared of my own shadow to even see friends outside of work, not that I had many left. Maybe I should just take the proverbial bull by the horns and enjoy my second chance at life. Wait until I tell my brother this holiday has done just that; I'll never hear the end of it. I can hear the *I told you so* already.

"I'm going to have a terrible head in the morning, mixing all of these drinks."

I can't remember the last alcoholic drink I had. Someone my age should be able to say I can't remember the last time I didn't have a drink.

"Good at the time though, right?"

"Right. A great start to my holiday. How long have you lived out here?"

I change the topic to something I've wanted to ask all night, but the lack of liquid courage kept my lips sealed. Now, the alcohol is fuelling my loose lips and I'm not scared to ask questions.

"I've been coming out to Bulgaria for about five years. I've only been living and running The Ranch since 2017. I can't imagine my life anywhere else now. I love it out here in the peak season. We're far enough away from the hustle and bustle of Sunny Beach, but close enough if we want the nightlife and shops."

I nod. It must be good to have your life all wrapped up with a pretty little bow. I've been existing and have no idea what life has in store for me. "What do you do when the season finishes? Do you stay here?"

"I stay here until about late October, early November. But then I do a bit of travelling for myself. I go home and visit my family in Italy, and then in late February, early March, I come back to the Bulgarian mountains and do some skiing, before I return here in April."

I nod in awe of this man having his life in order. "Sounds amazing. I wondered about your names since you have Scottish accents."

Giovani turns more on his side to face me. "My parents are from Italy. I was born in Scotland. My parents had their own chain of restaurants called Mama Bella. They retired about eight years ago and returned to Italy not long after. It's hard to lose the Scottish accent, not that I'd want to. Scotland is more my home than Italy ever was."

"Scotland is a beautiful place," I agree.

"What about yourself? You spend all your time in Scotland?"

I nod. I suddenly feel dull compared to Giovani. "I get the school holidays off since I'm a teacher, so I do get the opportunity to travel and visit different places. I just haven't had that luxury lately."

"I'm sorry to hear that."

"Don't be. My life is starting all over again this summer, and who knows what will happen next? I might get that travelling bug again."

I feel proud of myself for looking to the future instead of just living day by day, stuck in the past.

"Well, here's to the future." Giovani holds up his bottle of beer and I knock my Daiquiri glass against his and giggle.

I don't know how many of these cocktails I've had, but I have a warm feeling floating all over my body. I like it. It makes me feel carefree. The most carefree I've been in such a long time.

"Your turn." Lucca throws his arms around my shoulders and takes my glass from me. "Come on, Harl. Don't let the team down. You can't come here and not sing."

"No. No. Nope. I can't sing. Gio, help me!" I protest, but my trusted friend just holds his hands up and lets his brother man handle me up onto the stage.

It's a stark contrast to the way I felt shaking Lucca's hand just a short couple of hours ago. Now, I'm up singing with him, enjoying his company, not flinching when he touches my bare skin.

"I got you, Harls. We can make a fool of ourselves together. This is Bulgaria. Everyone is too happy to care about the Scottish person singing terribly on karaoke. They probably don't even understand you. Everyone is an amazing singer here."

As the melody of *I Got You Babe* floats through the air, I feel myself swaying to the tune.

No one will remember me tomorrow. I'll be going home in a few weeks where no one will ever see me again. I can make a fool of myself if I want to.

***

Who would have thought cobbled streets would be a fucker to walk on when you're intoxicated? I feel like a toddler learning to walk again.

I'm sandwiched in between Lucca and Gio. I don't know who's worse, me or Lucca. I'm glad I'm not alone, and Gio is taking our crazy drunkenness in his stride. He hasn't once treated us like we're embarrassing him or acting ridiculous.

"Back to Gio's for a nightcap," yells Lucca.

"Oh, no. I can't do that. I've put you both out enough tonight," I protest.

"Nonsense. Tell her, Gio. We'll make sure she gets back to the hotel safely."

"As much as it kills me to agree with Lucca, he's right. My house is just down the road from here. Five minutes from the hotel. I'll get you back to your room in one piece."

"You have coffee?" I ask boldly.

"Only the best coffee in Bulgaria," Gio states proudly.

"Okay. You have a deal."

The intoxicated me has no filter or ability to tell the devil on my shoulder to behave. I'm quite happy to rebel against my usual shy self. It has taken me long enough to stick the middle finger up to life.

We stop outside large iron gates. Gio types in a code on the panel and they open to let us through. The top of the house is on stilts and it's stunning. I don't know what I expected, but this wasn't it. It's like something you see in a magazine.

"You have a beautiful house."

"Thanks. Come on. The lady wants coffee."

And that's what we do. Entering Giovani's house was peaceful and quiet. Even the surrounding areas are tranquil for a holiday hotspot. We walk upstairs to get into his main living area. It's bright and spacious, fit for a king.

"Can I tempt you with something stronger than coffee, m'lady?" asks Lucca.

I sit down on the couch and wave my hands offendedly. "Absolutely not. I've drunk more alcohol today than I have in…" I pause and think about the last time I had a drink. "Well, such a long time."

I won't be transported to the time when tea and coffee was the only thing I could drink.

"You're on holiday, enjoy it." Lucca sits down opposite me with a bottle of beer in his hands. "I might be a little delicate tomorrow, too." He raises his bottle in the air a little too hard and some sloshes out of the top over his hand.

"Ye think?" I laugh and slip off my shoes. It surprises me how at home I feel. "I'll be dying tomorrow. I'll probably lose a day of my holiday, but I've had fun tonight."

"You only live once, dolly. What's one day when you've had a great night?"

And there hasn't been a truer word spoken. I'm done just existing. I don't want to be one of those people who live a full life and have nothing to show for it. I don't want to live until old age, and no one knows who I am. I want to make my mark on the world. I want to show people what I'm capable of.

"So, plans tomorrow, troops?" asks Gio as he approaches me with a large coffee mug in his hand.

"Thank you. I plan on exploring the area. Anywhere you suggest?"

I inhale the coffee like I need it to live. It's the best thing I've smelled all damn day. It even beats my sea view at dinner time.

"You need to check out Michael's Eco bar. It's along a wee alley at the back of the hotel. It's in a little hidey hole. It's an amazing place. You need to be there for it opening at twelve p.m., because people come from all over Bulgaria just to see it."

"Why is it called Eco Bar? Is it eco-friendly?"

"Something like that. It is all manmade, like a cave. Once you're inside, it opens up and there are pools of water, trees, and little booths where you can have a refreshing drink. The best bit is the little turtles that swim around you."

"Real turtles?" I ask excitedly.

"Absolutely real. You can't be in Old Nessebar without seeing it. If you meet me in the hotel lobby tomorrow morning about 11.30, I'll give you directions. It's pretty hard to find if you don't know where it is. When I'm out in the village shopping, I get asked so many times where it is. I should wear an arrow attached to me saying, *Michael's Eco Bar this way.*"

"Wow! Now I'm excited to see it. I'm fairly sure I'll be like the walking dead, though."

"Michael's is lovely and cool. The best place to be in the scorching heat. I live here, but the beauty of Old Nessebar and places like Michael's never gets old. I guarantee by the end of your holiday you won't want to leave, and you'll return year after year just to see things grow and become bigger and better."

"Now I know why my brother sent me here. He knows me too well. I like history and exploring new areas. I like seeing different things."

"He sounds like a good guy." Giovani folds his legs underneath himself and now I feel like he's towering over me, but in a good way. He doesn't intimidate me or make me feel nervous, which is good.

"He's a good guy. Just annoys the life out of me with his protective ways."

"I know the feeling of annoying brothers," Giovani points over to a now snoring Lucca. He reaches over and takes the bottle of beer from him before it spills all over the place. I can't help but laugh at him.

I lean my head back on the cushions and sigh. "Lucca's a good guy, too, Gio. He's funny."

"I'll remind you that you said that at the end of your holiday. Now he's found a drinking buddy, you'll never get peace."

"I don't mind. It will be good to have some company while I'm here. I thought I'd be spending the four weeks on my own. I'm not really big on socialising or getting to know new people. In fact, I'm socially awkward around people full stop."

"I would never have guessed. You did amazingly well to keep up with us tonight."

"I'll take that as a compliment. But all good things must come to an end." I sit forward. "Do you mind pointing me in the right direction to get back?"

"Nope. I can do one better than that. I'll walk you back. I wouldn't dream of letting you walk the streets at this hour on your own. I love this country, but there is the odd bad apple that wouldn't hesitate to take advantage of a woman walking alone."

I look down at my watch and gasp. "Oh my, it's three a.m.! I'm sorry to keep you up so late."

I'm shocked that I was so distracted tonight that the dangers of being out and about in a strange country never once entered my head.

"Don't be. I've had the best evening in such a long time. Come on, beautiful. Let's get you home for some sleep."

I put my mug down on the table then lift my shoes and put them in my bag. I'm going home barefoot, my party piece. I'm not a fan of shoes at all. I'm always barefoot at home. I think that might have come from my time with Martin, because I always had to be fully dressed from the moment I got up to the moment I went to bed, shoes and all. It's pleasurable now to have that freedom of choice, and I choose to be free of shoes.

We leave his house and walk down the street and turn slightly left. His hotel is sitting on the corner of the square. There are still people walking around, but not as many as earlier this evening.

"It's so easy to get lost here. All the streets look the same."

"Just remember, most streets always lead back to this square. You find the square; you find the hotel."

"Handy to know. I'm terrible with directions."

"I'll bear that in mind." He turns and winks at me as we enter the hotel lobby. "Well, I've had a good evening, Harleigh."

"Me too, Gio. I guess it's goodbye."

"I'll settle for goodnight." He leans in and places a kiss on my cheek.

I thought I would have frozen, fainted, or freaked out at the contact, but I didn't. I smile brightly at him, nod, and say, "Goodnight, Giovani."

I turn around as quick as my tired, drunken legs will take me. The concierge holds the lift doors open for me and I press level two for my room. I lift my hand and wave to Giovani as the doors close. We never take our eyes off one another until we're out of sight. Even then, my eyes don't leave the spot they were looking at through closed doors.

I exit the lift and make my way to my room. I take out my phone and type a message to my brother.

Gavin – I had an amazing night. Thank you for sending me here.

He's going to know I'm drunk by that text, because I never text with such enthusiasm. I push through my room door and stumble inside, making sure I'm secure with the door locked. I just hope I can sleep in this strange room alone.

A moment later, my phone rings in my hand. I answer it quickly, trying not to disturb any other guests, and lie down on my bed in an extremely unladylike position.

"Do you never sleep?" I ask my brother.

"Time difference. It's only the back of one here. I take it you're just home."

"Yip. I'm a tad tipsy."

"I gathered as much. I didn't think I'd hear from you at this time of morning otherwise. Did you go out alone, or have you made new friends?"

"New friends. The owner of this hotel is Scottish. Him and his brother kept me company tonight. I've had one too many cocktails, but it was so much fun. I even sang on karaoke; can you believe that?" I giggle at the memory.

"I'm glad you're having a good time, honey. It's good to hear you so happy."

"Oh, no brotherly talk about being out with strange men?"

He laughs. "No. You're a big girl. But if anyone hurts you, I'll be on the first flight to kick some arse."

I shrug and close my eyes. "Okay. I need sleep. I love you, Gav."

"I love you too, Harl. Sleep tight."

I hang up my phone, toss it on the bed beside me, and curl into the pillows. My tired, aching body is in heaven. This is only the first day. By the end of this holiday I won't want to go back to my boring, normal life. I might need another holiday to get over this one.

Chapter 6

Giovani

I look at the time and it's eleven a.m. Lucca is still passed out on the couch. I've tried to rouse him several times, but it's a pointless task with his drunken arse. I'll let him sleep it off, and rather than give Harleigh directions, I'll accompany her to Michael's Eco Bar. I'd much rather get to know Harleigh better than babysit my brother, as much as I love him.

I don't know what it is about this woman that has gotten under my skin, but I want to spend time with her. I want to get to know her, warts and all. I know she has a lot of stories to tell; it's written all over her features when she's around people, but that isn't frightening me away. I think it's encouraging me to get to know her more, which is out of the norm for me.

Since my ex fucked me over about three years ago, women have been off my agenda, period. I've had my fair share of heartache and misery, but being out here in Bulgaria makes everything happy and cheerful. It covers over my history and allows me to enjoy my life. Spending time with holiday makers, making their holiday memorable, sun, sea, and cocktails, it keeps my mind busy. Well, that was until Harleigh walked into my hotel and made me question what I want out of life.

I grab my phone, wallet, and keys. I'm on a high to get to Harleigh, spend the day with her, showing her places I love, and I just love everything about Bulgaria. I won't get fed up of showing her the sights. I'm pretty sure we can cram so much into four weeks if she wants a tour guide.

I exit my house and enter the street. I practically jog around to my hotel. It's too hot for any kind of exercise, but I don't care. The streets are already busy, people exploring, buying trinkets, and soaking up the sun. It's an instant feel-good factor. Well, it is for me. I guess that's why I set up home here.

I walk into my hotel foyer. People are laughing, joking, and getting ready to head out into the sun. I acknowledge people that pass me, wave to my receptionist, and instantly spot Harleigh sitting in the sunroom. Sunglasses down on her eyes, book open, hair tied back in a ponytail. It's a stark contrast to the put together woman I saw yesterday. Today, she seems more comfortable, relaxed even. It's good to see. I'm wondering how much of that relaxed look has got hangover written all over it. I'm surprised she's up at all. It's good that she isn't like my brother - still dying.

I approach her quietly, taking in her beauty. She's totally different to any other woman I know, because even though she's stunning, she doesn't realise how beautiful she is. She acts so blasé, which I love about her.

"Good morning." I smile brightly.

Harleigh looks up and smiles back at me. "Good morning, Gio. You look… okay." She giggles, and it's the best sound in the world. "No one would think I'm a teacher and editor. That came out wrong. What I meant to say is that you look good considering how I feel. I woke up with a herd of elephants dancing in my head. Alcohol is the devil."

I chuckle and sit down beside her on the spare seat. "I don't get hangovers very often. My brother, on the other hand... I couldn't even wake him this morning. I did think about turning the hose onto him, but a) I don't think I could listen to his childish moaning, and b) he's still lying in my living room. The cleaning up would be left to me, and I'd much rather be showing you the sights."

"I know how Lucca feels. I'm not used to drinking so much, but it was good to let my hair down. I'm not sure I've had the best idea sitting in a glass room when it's so warm outside." We both laugh. "So, you said about directing me to an Eco Bar."

"I did. But, since I have time on my hands, if you like, I can accompany you there and show you some sights."

Harleigh looks at me. She looks like a deer caught in headlights. I didn't mean to startle her; it was the last thing I intended to do.

"Only if you don't mind," I push forward.

"I don't want to put you out." She smiles weakly at me.

"I wouldn't be here if I didn't want to be."

"Okay," she says, a little too much like if she doesn't say okay, she'd run in the opposite direction. "Do I need to do anything or wear anything specific for an Eco Bar?"

I shake my head. "Nope. As you are is perfect. Are you ready?"

"I am. I'm really looking forward to seeing this bar. I looked it up on Facebook and the pictures look amazing."

"Pictures do it no justice."

I stand up and wait for Harleigh to put her book in her bag, grab her hat, and stand up. I hold my hand out to her without thinking. She looks on edge again, as if warring with herself whether she should hold my hand or not. Yesterday, when I met her, she was like a skittish mouse, but last night she was more relaxed and herself. I'm hoping that in time she will relax more and realise I'm not out to hurt her in any way. I want to see the person I saw last night all the time. That's what I will set out to do.

"I won't bite, I promise," I smile at her.

She nods and holds her hand out to mine. I see her hesitate, but she finally takes it. I could have taken her hand for her, but I don't want to push her to do things she's clearly not ready to do. I will never push any woman; it isn't in my nature.

We walk through the hotel slowly.

"Good morning, Giovani," says Horatio, my doorman. "Beautiful day for exploring." He raises his brows and lifts his hat to me and Harleigh.

"It is indeed, Horatio. This is Harleigh. Harleigh, this is Horatio. If you ever need anything when I'm not around, just give him a shout."

"Anytime." Horatio holds his hand out to Harleigh. "I never sleep. You'd think I live on this door. Come find me anytime and I'll help you."

"Thank you. Everyone is so kind." Harleigh smiles and tightens her grip on my hand. It's as if she's a little nervous of Horatio. I'm not sure if she's even aware that she did it.

"Well, we'll be on our way." I walk away from my doorman and Harleigh follows at my side. "Horatio is harmless. He'll take care of you."

I don't know why I feel the need to make Harleigh feel at ease all the time, it just comes naturally. I like to help people when I can, but Harleigh is different and I can't put my finger on what makes her unique.

"I get the feeling he has a story."

"He does. He lost his wife, Deeanna, of forty years about eighteen months ago. He practically lives in the hotel. I don't mind. I pay him extra and it keeps him active and possibly alive, because I think he'd give up and end up with Deeanna if he was at home all the time."

"No kids?"

"Two sons. They both live in Sofia. They visit frequently. Nothing will ever make him leave Nessebar. This is his home."

"I get it. I'm a hopeless romantic. He probably feels a connection to Deeanna here."

"I thought you might believe in love at first sight and romance." I smile and navigate us along the cobbled streets.

"You don't?" Harleigh turns to me, still holding my hand, studying every move I make. I like this inquisitive side of her.

"I think I once did. I have Italian in my blood. It's a part of the Italian dream. Love, family, happiness."

"So, what made you lose that faith in love and happiness?"

"Life, I think. I've been thrown a few curveballs. Let's just say that relationships have never been my strong point."

I speak openly and freely. I don't feel like I need to hide who I am from Harleigh. She's genuinely interested in me as a person, and it may just make her relax if she knows everything about me.

Harleigh nods and turns back to face the way we're walking. "You and me both. People suck at times, huh?"

I nod. "They do. I'm guessing you have a story to tell too?"

She nods sombrely. "I do. I think we all do. I tell my pupils and authors that everyone has a story to tell."

I don't want to push her. If she wants to tell me her life story, she will in her own time. I don't plan on going anywhere.

"Oh, wow." She looks over at an old shop attached to someone's house. A black Labrador is sitting outside with his owner. "Are all the shops like this here?"

"Pretty much. Bulgaria is an old town. Old blood. People live to a ripe old age here. Looking at it you'd think people were living in the dark ages, but it works for them. Would you like to have a look inside?"

"Do we have time?"

"Absolutely."

I lead the way into the shop. We acknowledge the owner sitting at the door. He remains sitting in the sun.

"Do they make everything themselves?"

"Some people do. Pottery and lace are high amongst the things people make here."

She picks up a large, what I would call, casserole bowl. It's brightly painted in orange and browns.

"Do you mind if I buy a few things?" she asks.

"No, go ahead. The hotel isn't far from here if we need to make a stop off to take things back."

The bright smile on Harleigh's face is infectious. Watching her pick up some trinkets should be boring, but I find everything about her intriguing. I offer to take her items to allow her to browse at her leisure. I don't mind shopping; besides, the inside of these small shops are cooler than outside. It's no hardship being here with a beautifully kind woman.

"My mum will love these dishes." She picks up a smaller casserole dish at the front of the store where the owner is sitting. She hands him everything and he calculates the cost in his head.

"Eighty-three lev."

Harleigh hands over the cash and I take her bag from the owner.

"Keep the change." She waves at the old guy.

Seven lev isn't a lot to us, but to Bulgarians who rely on tourists, it is.

"I could get used to this place. Everyone is so extremely kind."

I take her hand and we walk along the side street slowly.

"You won't come across many unpleasant Bulgarians. They live for the summer season and enjoy meeting the tourists. This is Michael's Eco-bar," I point to my right where a small shack is situated. There are already some people queueing up for it opening at twelve o'clock.

"Wow! It looks very... pokey." She smiles.

"It is. But it's magical inside. Just you wait until you see it. People come from all over Bulgaria just to capture it. People queue up all day to get in."

"I don't think I've ever been this excited to see a bar before." She giggles infectiously.

The door opens to the bar and the people in front of us head inside. I take Harleigh's hand and lead her down the small, narrow steps. It's like Aladdin's cave inside. I can't wait to see her expression.

"Good afternoon," says a young girl as she allows us to enter and hands us a drinks menu.

"Oh. My. God."

I look over my shoulder and catch Harleigh's expression as she gazes around the small cave. I take her out back, up a few stairs and over a little bridge to a booth where we can still catch some sun, watch the turtles, and enjoy a drink.

"This is amazing. I..." she sits down beside me and watches the small turtles swim in the little pool. "I honestly feel speechless."

"It's something else, right?"

"It's beautiful."

I put my menu down on the table. I should know it like the back of my hand. "The cocktails are to die for as well."

"Well, since you're the expert, I'll let you decide for me."

The waitress walks over to us to take our order. "Can we have two of your most asked for cocktails? We'll let you decide."

I'm not good at deciding for people, so I'll take the easy way out and let the waitress decide for us. To be quite honest, there probably aren't many I haven't tried. Lucca and I like coming here for a little escape. My parents love it. They rave about it to friends and family. My brother is the drinks picker. He knows all about what to mix with what. I can see him working in a cocktail bar one day.

"This is breath-taking."

The waitress places two tall glasses down in front of us. The green liquid looks cool and enticing.

"Thank you." Harleigh addresses the waitress. She lifts her glass, looks at it curiously, and raises it to me. "Cheers."

I clink my glass with hers and watch in amusement as she takes a delicate sip of her drink.

"Oh, it tastes just like juice. I did wonder if I'd be sick from the sight or smell of another alcoholic beverage so soon today, but I could get used to this."

I chuckle at her innocence. "I always thought teachers would have to be silent alcoholics with everything they face daily."

Harleigh turns her attention from the small turtle sitting beside her to me. "It's not so bad. Yes, we have the odd little monster that pushes buttons, but overall, I enjoy my job. I missed it when I didn't work."

"Lady of leisure, huh?"

Harleigh's face falls slightly and she gulps deeply. I wish I could take back those words. "Something like that. It isn't a time of my life that I like to relive. Let's just say I'm a different person now."

I raise my glass and nod at her softly. "We all have parts of our life that challenge us. I think it makes us stronger."

"I'm working on it. So, what's on your agenda for today?"

I smile warmly at her brief change of subject. I'm happy with that, because I'm getting used to the carefree look on her face. I didn't like the sombre look a moment ago.

"Well, if you like, I'd like to take you to lunch. I know the perfect restaurant on the harbour if you like seafood."

"I love seafood."

And just like that, the excitement that radiates from Harleigh is back again. The scary part is that I could get used to having her around, and that thought terrifies me.

"I know I say this all the time, but I don't want to put you out. You must have work to do."

I shake my head. "I always have time to spare. I'd only be stuck in my office if I was back at the hotel. I'd much rather have a day off with you. Besides, what's the point of being the boss if I can't make my own rules?" I shrug and we both smile.

"Okay. On one condition." She holds one finger up and points it delicately at my chest.

"Name it."

"I pay for lunch."

"Oh." I cringe. I don't know what I was expecting, but that wasn't it. "It's a hard bargain, because I've been brought up to pay, but I think I can stretch to you paying for *one* lunch." I emphasise the word one.

"Then you have a date, Giovani. Well, not a date. You know what I mean."

Harleigh's flustered look makes me reach over and take her hand. "I like the sound of a lunch date. It's been so long since I had a date."

"Okay." She tucks an imaginary strand of hair behind her ear and smiles at me.

Harleigh is the opposite of the type of woman I've been attracted to before. She seems kind, quiet, independent. No woman has ever asked to pay for our lunch date. Maybe I've been attracting the wrong type of woman. Eurgh, what am I saying? Harleigh is only here on holiday. She won't like the lifestyle I lead. I need to enjoy this time while it lasts because it will end very quickly. Life will return to normal in a couple of weeks and we'll both be back to square one.

Chapter 7

Harleigh

Today has been a lovely day. As promised, Giovani has been the perfect tour guide. I've had fun. In fact, I've had nothing but fun since the moment I arrived in Bulgaria. It's refreshing to feel light and untroubled. I've not had to worry about a thing since I left Scotland, and I really like that. It's amazing how stress free I've been since I arrived here. It's good for the soul and my mental health.

When Giovani and I arrived back at the hotel, he got called away to take care of something in his office. I found myself gravitating to the wonderful pool area. I ordered the cocktail of the day, found a sun lounger, took out my book, and started reading. The gentle chatter and laughter from the other holiday makers lull me into a relaxed state. I don't know how long I've been sitting out here, but the sweat covering my body is a good indicator that I should probably cool off before I have to head out for dinner.

"Drinking already. You're a badass." Lucca plonks himself down opposite me and lounges back on the vacant sun lounger.

"Your brother said you were dead this morning." I laugh.

He still looks a little green around the gills, but he's up, walking and talking, so that's a good sign.

"That was probably an accurate description. I felt like death warmed up when I did open my eyes. How was your day? I hope Gio treated you right."

"Like a perfect gentleman. Today was lovely. Just what I needed after our wild night."

"Speaking of wild, do you fancy another wild evening?"

I groaned. "I'm not a big drinker. Another night like last night and I'll be digging my own grave."

"I was being sarcastic. My head could not stand another wild evening too soon. My idea of wild is a barbecue, a few beers, and some decent company at my brother's pool."

I think over everything Lucca is saying. I don't want to intrude. "Wouldn't Gio mind? He's been more than courteous since I arrived. He doesn't have to babysit me."

"Nonsense. Gio likes you. I like you, like an annoying sister."

"Wow! Thanks, bro." I mock and throw the strap of my bag over my shoulder. "If Giovani doesn't mind then that sounds like a plan."

"If Giovani doesn't mind what?" His voice makes me jump.

Thankfully, my big sunglasses are hiding my gaze as it travels up and down his toned body.

"I was just asking Harls if she fancies coming over to your house tonight for a few beers and a barbecue."

"Definitely. And to help you make your mind up, I'll cook so you don't end up with food poisoning."

Lucca sits bolt upright and holds his hand over his chest. "I can cook, you're just a cheeky arsehole."

I giggle at the two brothers. They remind me of my own siblings – fun to be around.

"What do you say, Harls? You game for trying my cooking?"

"Absolutely. I'll bring some drinks. What do you both like?"

"My brother owns a hotel. He has a cellar full. Just bring yourself." Lucca jumps off the lounger and punches Giovani's shoulder. "See you later, bro."

Giovani shakes his head at his brother and sits down on the lounger Lucca just vacated.

"He keeps you on your toes."

"He's going to be the death of me." We both chuckle. "You're a lovely shade of brown already."

"Good. The lobster look doesn't suit me. So, about tonight, do you really not mind me tagging along?"

"No, of course I don't. I was coming to find you to see if you would let me take you to dinner, but Lucca's idea sounds good. I'll just have to get you to agree to dinner another night."

My cheeks heat even more. "I'll hold you to that. I should get out of this heat, go for a shower, and get dressed for tonight. Thank you for today. I really enjoyed it."

"No thanks necessary. I'll see you tonight, Miss Harleigh."

"That you will." We both stand up together. "Bye, Giovani."

"Bye."

I turn away and practically skip away. I've never had as much excitement or so many plans in my life. I'm all work and no play, but I'm realising that makes a boring life.

Just being away from Scotland has made a big difference to the way I view things. I'm not looking over my shoulder, wondering what's going to happen next, or what will become of my existence. After this holiday I'm going to be changing the way I look at life full stop. I'm going to live for the moment and enjoy every single minute. I'm going to make plans and stick to them. I won't let the past dictate my life any longer.

Maybe this holiday will open up my mind to lots of new possibilities.

Chapter 8

Harleigh

You'd think I was going for dinner with the Queen the way I'm primping and preening myself. Gio and Lucca won't care what I'm wearing. They don't seem like the kind of guys to care about the attire I choose, and I like that. Martin always had a say in what I wore. I wasn't allowed to dress like a woman of my twenty-seven years. I dressed more like my grandma. Well, my grandma probably dressed more fashionably than I ever did during my relationship with Martin.

I throw on a long black maxi-dress over my swimsuit. I'm not sure if I'll have the confidence to use Giovani's pool, but it looks better to wear a swimsuit than a bra. It feels better too. I've always been well-endowed; forgoing a bra is never something I can do unless I'm in my pyjamas. It's something I like doing now, because when I was around my ex, he used to make sure I knew how much he detested my curves. It was something he could do anytime of the day, around people or on our own. Even a year on, I still hear his snarky comments on repeat.

I stand up straighter, push my chest out proudly, and ruffle my fingers through my hair. I like this *don't give a toss* attitude.

I grab the bottle of prosecco Giovani had sent to my room on my first day here. I'll never drink it alone, so I'm as well taking it with me, and my new holiday buddies can help me devour it. I've never been to someone's house for dinner without taking a small gift; it's compulsory in my rule book. I grab my small bag, place the bottle inside, and leave my room. Soft music is echoing up the stairs from the lounge.

"Good evening, Miss," says Horatio.

I can see what he means about never being away from this door. He was here when Giovani and I left at eleven a.m., and he's still here at eight p.m.

"Good evening, Horatio."

"Dinner time?"

"It is. The sea air and sun are making me eat like a horse."

We both exchange a chuckle and I leave the hotel lobby. I'm pretty sure Horatio didn't really understand everything I said, but he's always pleasant to me.

The moment I leave the hotel steps, the evening heat hits me. There isn't a bit of air at all. It feels just like it did this afternoon, only more humid. I could get used to living like this. I think the jet set lifestyle would suit my newfound personality.

I walk along the cobbled street with no cares in the world. It's a good feeling. People are sitting in restaurants, browsing the shops, and enjoying their families. It's nice to see so many different nationalities in one area.

I turn the corner into Giovani's street, and up in the distance, his house is glowing higher than all the other buildings in the area. It's like it's on a pedestal. All the other houses are dull in comparison. It's an amazing house. I can see the beauty of it today in the dusk light. I'm also not inebriated by alcohol, so I can take in the elegance that radiates from the building alone.

I slip through the small gate off to the side, instead of the double gates that allow cars to pass through into the driveway. I can't take my eyes off the house.

"Are you just going to gawp or are you coming up?" Lucca brushes past me with his arms filled with bags.

"Let me help you." But he's walking at speed up the steps towards the house. I follow swiftly behind him, around the side of the house, and out into the back garden. Giovani is off to the far side, cooking on the grill. The barbecue aroma fills my senses and my stomach growls. I walk over to him and take out the bottle of prosecco. He turns just as I approach him. His smile lights up his face. He's like a model. His shorts sit delicately on his hips, his polo shirt is untucked, but it's his bare feet that make me swoon.

Eurgh! I need to get a grip if I'm going to survive this dinner. I have absolutely no idea what's wrong with me.

"You made it." He leans in and places a soft kiss on my cheek.

Instead of recoiling at his touch, I relish in it.

"I did. I brought this."

"You didn't need to, but thank you. What can I get you to drink?"

"Oh, whatever you have open. Don't go to any trouble."

"Harleigh," he asks sternly, but not in an uncomfortable way. "What would *you* like?"

I feel my cheeks doing their signature party piece. "Erm, a white wine would be nice if you have it, but if not…"

He cuts me off by lifting my chin. "I have everything, but if I didn't, I would have sent Lucca to get some. It's the least he could do since I'm feeding his arse."

We both laugh and I follow Giovani into his house. "Don't you need to keep an eye on what's cooking?"

"It will be okay for a few minutes."

We enter his large kitchen from the patio area. Lucca is chopping and dicing some salad ingredients. He looks comfortable.

"Ignore Gordon Ramsay over there. He's a crabit arse when he's in the kitchen."

I giggle at Giovani as Lucca continues to slice and dice. He doesn't even acknowledge us in his space. Giovani hands me over a wine glass and pops the cork on the bottle.

"Would you like some ice?"

"Oh, yes, please. It feels hotter than the Sahara Desert right now."

"You'll get used to it. Give it a few days and you'll love the hot weather. You'll never want to leave and return to boring Scottish weather."

"Oh, I'm already there. I could get used to the easy, carefree lifestyle."

I follow Giovani back outside and he pulls over a chair to the grill. "Have a seat. Take the weight off, relax, and have some fun."

You can tell that Giovani and Lucca are used to being in the hospitality trade. They're always so friendly and happy to entertain people. I'm just glad my brother found the right hotel, because my trip would have been very different without this pair of brothers keeping me entertained.

It's crazy, because just a few days ago, the thought of being around strange men terrified me. Yet, here I am, living life and enjoying it. There is just something about Lucca and Giovani that makes me relaxed. The apprehension of my past is still knocking in the background, but with them, I can keep it in the background. I won't let it put a dampener on the first friendship I've made in years.

"I've probably told you this a dozen times, but you have a beautiful home."

Giovani takes a drink of his beer. "Thank you. I love it here. I wish I could live here all year round, but it isn't really practical once the season ends. It's like a ghost town come November."

"It's hard to picture that, but I guess it's like all the tourist areas, huh?"

"It gives me time to visit family and explore other areas of the world that interest me. You like to travel?"

I nod. "I do. Or I did. This is my first real holiday in a few years. I'm going to make it my mission to visit different places again. I get enough holidays to do so."

"Favourite place so far?"

"Oh..." I think carefully, because I've enjoyed a few places. "Italy, I think. Or Paris. I loved both of those places."

"My parents will love you for saying Italy."

"Nothing beats Italian food, wine, hospitality, and countryside. It's breath-taking."

"I'm sweating like a whore in a brothel. That kitchen is sweltering," says Lucca as he approaches the table, placing plates down.

I can't stop laughing. He has a way with words and doesn't care what people think about him. Maybe that's why I like him so much.

"Ignore my brother. He's a nightmare." Giovani laughs and shakes his head. "Come and stand at the grill. You'll know what it's like to be hot and sweaty."

"Nah, you've got that, bro. I don't want to steel your crown."

Lucca sits down at the table and opens the parasol. It covers the whole table and then some. It's huge, but it looks so cool and enticing."

"Come over, Harls. You won't burn over here… or melt."

I do as asked of me and sit opposite Lucca, but still facing Giovani, because I hate having my back to people.

"You look beautiful tonight, doesn't she, Gio?"

"Absolutely. She always does," I hear Giovani mutter, but I don't think I was supposed to hear the last bit.

"Gio makes the best steaks. Just wait until you taste them."

My stomach takes that moment to growl loudly. I hold it and smile. "Excuse my stomach. I've eaten more since I arrived here than I have in the last month."

"Here, try my version of Shopska salad. Cucumber, peppers, onion, the best tomatoes around, covered in feta cheese. It's amazing."

"It sounds it. Is it Bulgarian?"

"Bulgaria's speciality. Try it."

I accept the bowl that Lucca hands me and I spoon some onto a side plate. Oh my God, the smell of fresh vegetables is amazing. I feel my mouth watering at the thought of all the different textures hitting my palate.

I moan as the mixture tantalises my taste buds. "It's delicious."

"One of my favourite dishes here," Gio calls over to us.

I feel like a starved woman because I haven't stopped eating since it hit my plate.

"I can see why. Those tomatoes are the best I've ever tasted."

"I guarantee you won't look at another tomato the same way again after eating a Bulgarian tomato," says Lucca, very sure of himself.

I devour the salad on my plate and feel content. At least eating salad is healthy. I won't have to worry about any crash diets when I get home.

Tonight gets off to a good start; good company, good food and wine, and the best location ever.

What more could I ask for?

***

"As much as I've loved tonight, this party animal needs some beauty sleep," says Lucca. He raises his bottle, stands up, and leaves the table. "Night, bro."

"You have a good family." I take a sip of the wine I've been nursing for a while.

"Yeah, they're not too bad. What about you? Brothers, you said, right?"

Gio turns onto his side to face me, his ankle crossed under his thigh, and our knees brush against one another. He looks comfortable.

"Two brothers. Older brothers. They're very protective."

"Typical brotherly role. And your parents?"

"Both retired. My mother is a retired English professor. My dad is a retired builder."

"They say opposites attract."

"Indeed. My mum and dad are like chalk and cheese, but I love them. I can't imagine life without them."

"And no boyfriend or husband?"

"Nope. Young, free, and very single. *Very single*," I repeat nervously.

"I find it hard to believe that a beautiful, talented young woman would be single."

"Charmer." I tuck a strand of hair behind my ear. "I was with someone. Engaged, to be more precise."

"I get the feeling there is more to this story."

I nod weakly. I've never really spoken about my ordeal to anyone other than my family, but there is something about Gio that makes me want to tell him. I turn to face him.

"I was abused, physically and mentally, by my fiancé. That's why I'm single. I got away. I've spent the last twelve months trying to get my life back to normal, or as normal as can be after everything that happened. That's why my brother booked this holiday. He thought that sun, sea, and cocktails would do me the world of good." I lift my glass and take a big gulp of wine.

I can feel the anxiety rushing through my veins. My heart is pounding in my chest. Tears appear in my eyes and I don't want to let my past consume me.

"I am so sorry that you've been through that." Gio reaches over and takes my hand. "No one should ever be treated badly, especially not by someone who should love and protect them. Some people are just arseholes. I'm glad you have family who helped get you through it. And never forget that I'm always here if you need an escape. Anytime, day or night."

"Thank you." I feel the heat in my cheeks rise. "I'm glad I decided to come on this adventure. And I'm sorry about being emotional."

"You never have to apologise for being upset around me, Harleigh."

I nod.

"Anyway, I bet your brother is mighty glad to hear that you're enjoying this trip."

"Yes. I'm just waiting for the 'I told you so,' speech." I roll my eyes and straighten my back.

"That's what brothers are for."

"So, I've shared my life story with you. Is there no Mrs Giovani?"

Giovani straightens up and takes in a deep breath. I can see the turmoil in his features.

"I had a fiancée as well. Let's just say that it ended badly. She left me high and dry, bled my accounts dry, and ran off with my best friend, Jack."

"Oh my God. I'm so sorry, Giovani. Was this a long time ago?"

"A few years ago now. I was lucky I had business accounts that only I could get into, otherwise all of this would have just been a pipedream."

"Gosh, I don't know what's wrong with some people. Her parents must be so proud." I shake my head in disgust.

"You're the first person, other than family, that I've told about her. I've always hid it from my present."

"I'm glad you did. And, for what it's worth, you're the first person I've confided my life secrets to."

"So, no more skeletons in the closet, no bodies under your floorboards?" Giovani smiles wickedly.

"No, not humans anyway. When I was a child, I made my dad bury my goldfish in the garden. My parents still live in the same house." I giggle. "Does that count?"

I think the wine is finally going to my head.

"Poor goldfish. I'm pretty sure Lucca's goldfish got flushed down the toilet when he was four. He was upset with my mum and dad for weeks. It's a story my dad still shares to this day."

I laugh. I could just picture Lucca as a toddler, upset and in tears over his flushed away goldfish. He is just an adult-sized child now.

I sit back in my seat and tilt my head back to the night sky. It's like a totally different world here. There is a perfect combination of everything.

"It's so peaceful here. I can see why you love it so much."

"It's one of my favourite places to be. It doesn't feel like work. In fact, what are you doing tomorrow?"

"If you hadn't noticed, I'm kind of living day by day here. My plans and making routines have completely gone out the window, and I like it. I like being impulsive. Why? What did you have in mind?"

"I have a business property to see over in Sunny Beach. Maybe you can come with me. I'll drive us over, and then I can show you some of what Sunny Beach has to offer. I can throw in lunch if you give me your honest opinion."

"I can do that. Tomorrow sounds fabulous already."

"I'll pick you up at the hotel in the morning, say eleven?"

"Sounds good to me. Let me help you clear up before I go home."

"Nah, leave it. I'll get it later. Besides, I'm enjoying your company too much. If I walk you back to the hotel, I can spend more time with you."

"I'd like that." I smile brightly.

I honestly don't know what it is with Giovani, but he is making me feel things that I've never felt before. Is it lust? I'm not sure. I've never had a holiday romance, and I don't know if I'm the type of person to be with someone for a couple of weeks, go home, and forget all about them. That's not the type of person I am. Could I be, though?

I guess only time will tell.

***

Giovani walks me right to my room door tonight. He said he has something to do in his office so it's no bother. I rock back on my heels, feeling a little nervous. Giovani tilts my chin with his thumb and makes me look him in the eye.

"I don't like to see the unsettled look on your face. I've come to like the untroubled look. The one that looks like you're sticking your middle finger up to anyone who has wronged you over the years. And, just to let you know, there is absolutely nothing to be scared of when you're around me. I will protect you. Nothing and no one will ever hurt you or upset you when I'm around."

"I'm not scared of you, Giovani. I'm actually the most relaxed I've been in… such a long time." I breathe out a sigh of relief. "I like spending time with you. I never imagined I'd be here with someone like you. I thought I would have spent my full holiday hiding away at the pool, but you make me excited to start a new day."

"I'm glad to hear it, Harleigh. I like spending time with you too. And, just to set the record straight, that doesn't happen very often. After what happened to me, I knuckled down with work and built up this empire. I didn't let any women in. There is something different about you and I can't put my finger on it."

"Well, when you figure it out, be sure to let me know."

"What would you say if I said I needed to kiss you, right here, right now?"

My heart stutters in my chest. The excitement of what Giovani just said registers in my inebriated brain. Not that I'm drunk tonight. I've just got this warm fuzzy feeling floating through me.

"I'd say..." I look at Giovani's inviting mouth and part my lips slightly. "...I think I'd like that very much."

"Good." Giovani leans into me. "That's very good."

He leans in closer and captures my lips with his. Our mouths become one. His tongue delves into my soul, caresses every corner, and gives me everything he has. I've never been kissed like this before; I don't know if it's the wine or the kiss that's making me lightheaded. The ground underneath my feet feels like it's moving.

Gio parts from the kiss, leans his forehead against mine, and breathes heavily. My heart is pounding, my breathing is ragged, and my body feels like it's alive, with electricity zapping through me. I feel alive. How is that possible from one kiss?

"That was..." I pant. "Amazing."

"I'm glad to hear it. I'm going to bid you a goodnight, because if I kiss you like that once more, I'm afraid I won't be able to walk away without taking you into that room, ripping your clothes off, and worshipping every inch of you. I'll pick you up in the morning. Goodnight, Harleigh." He leans in and places the softest kiss to my lips then walks away from me.

Did that just happen? Did Giovani just kiss me like it was his last? Did I just about orgasm on this spot from one mind-blowing kiss?

The pinging of the elevator snaps me back to here and now. I rub my finger over my swollen lips and remember every glorious moment of the minute I just shared with Giovani. If that was one kiss, I can only imagine what anything else is like. I fish out my key card, open the door, and walk into my room in a daze.

I am fucked!

***

I've lay in bed and tossed and turned for hours. I'm finally feeling tired, but I can't get that kiss with Giovani out of my head. I liked it. No, if I'm honest with myself, I loved it. But there is this fear and anxiety coursing through my veins. Is it because I stepped out of my comfort zone tonight and let Giovani kiss me? Is it because I'm all over the place with being on holiday alone? I don't know, and trying to analyse every damn thing is making me worse.

One kiss. One kiss, and my head is a mess. I've never felt that way over one kiss before. Christ, I used to be terrified if Martin ever stepped too close to me, never mind put his lips on me. Saying that, in the latter weeks and months, he would more than likely put his hands on me than show me any kind of love and affection.

I close my eyes and try to ease this turmoil, but now I'm consumed by Giovani and Martin.

"You will never look at another man again. You will never smile at another man again. Do I make myself clear?" Martin spits as he holds my chin tightly in his hand.

Tonight, we were at a gala dinner for his work colleagues. I always smile and act courteous, and tonight was no different. I smiled a little longer at an elder man called Paul, and of course, this cretin had to see it.

"I was just being nice to your colleagues. I meant nothing by it. You have to believe me, Martin."

I'm not placating him because I like him. I'm doing it because I want to spare myself a few extra bruises.

"Why would I believe a lying slag like you?" He back hands me across the face and I hit my head on the wall behind me. "Get up those stairs, take off that make-up, and be ready for me coming to bed."

I hold my cheek and scurry away like a child being scolded by their parents. I wish he would have knocked me out or gone back out to be with his many whores who drop their knickers for him. Now I need to go upstairs and prepare myself for him and be ready for him to slip inside of me, have his wicked way with me, and then roll over and fall asleep. It's just going to be another night where I have to look like I'm enjoying myself or the sexual abuse will just get harder and more punishing.

I sit upright and bang my hands down on the mattress. I'm frustrated that I let that bloody vision take over me, tonight of all nights, when I'm thinking about Giovani and how much his touch thrilled and excited me.

Tonight is going to be a very long night.

Chapter 9

Giovani

I had to walk away from Harleigh last night, because I've never felt as turned on by a kiss in my life. Her body against mine, her soft lips and tongue, her breath against my mouth. It was like all my dreams come true. If I'd stayed one more moment, I would have turned into a sex mad maniac and had my way with her. I don't want to frighten her away, because I love spending time with her. Which is crazy, because I haven't spent time with a woman in over three years. Sure, I've slept with a couple, a man has needs, but they've never interested me in anything else. Harleigh is different though. She thrills and excites me. She makes me want more.

"Morning, bro. Did Harleigh get back to the hotel okay?"

"Yeah. I'm picking her up in an hour to go to Sunny Beach with me."

"You like her, huh?"

I nod. "I do. I can't explain it, but I really like her."

"Good. I'm over the fucking moon for you. You deserve some happiness, and Harleigh seems like a nice girl. It's about time you moved on, had some fun, and just kicked back. You work too hard."

"Kicked back? What's that, some sort of teen slang?"

"I'm down with the cool kids." Lucca makes a silly motion with his hands and fingers. I'm pretty sure the daft bugger forgets what age he is sometimes.

"I worry about you, bro. I really worry about you." I shake my head.

"Don't be daft. Get out of here, go and have some fun."

"I might just do that after I see the building for the new bar."

"I thought you were just sounding off some thoughts when you mentioned that last week."

"I was, I think. But, the more I think about it, Sunny Beach is where all the nightlife and tourists are. Sure, they come over here for Old Nessebar, but it's not a hot spot at night, unless you're older and wiser. It might make us a tidy profit."

"If you say so. I'll go along with whatever you want. You're the brains. Let me know how it goes."

I nod, pick up my keys, down my coffee, and leave the house. Today is going to be an extremely good day. I can feel it in my bones.

***

Walking into my hotel is always a proud moment. After my ex did what she did to me, I hit rock bottom. I was ashamed of the way things turned out. When I found out that she hadn't just slept with one person behind my back, I felt dirty and used. It was clear that she was only with me to see what she could get from me, or steal from me. Once I got away from it all, I didn't know what to do with my life. I felt like I was sinking into a deep, dark hole and there was little light for me to see a way out. I came out to Sunny Beach for a guys' holiday. An escape from reality; sun, sea, sex, and lots of drink. I did all of the above, but one day I took the little sea taxi from Sunny Beach Pier out to Nessebar. After walking around for hours, drinking the odd pint of lager to keep hydrated, shopping in the little shops, exploring the sights, I fell in love with the whole area. I sat in the square outside the hotel and looked up to the sky. When I straightened up my head, I saw the *For Sale* sign. The hotel needed some TLC, but I could picture myself here, owning the hotel, and enjoying the peak holiday season. I bought the hotel, hired Bulgarian contractors to do the work I needed, and opened for the next season. So, that pride I feel when walking inside this building comes from knowing how much of a dark place I was in, to finding the light and turning my life into something I love.

Walking out of the elevator is Harleigh. Her long, wavy hair is hanging around her shoulders today. Her sunglasses are perched on her head. Her body is encased in a short all in one playsuit. She looks like a model. Not that she would ever see herself like that. Her arsehole ex made a mark on her, and not just a physical mark, but a permanent mental mark, too. I'll do everything in my power to make her realise that she's smart, beautiful, and extremely kind. There is nothing negative I can say about her.

"Good morning." Harleigh breaks through my thoughts.

I clear my throat, lean in, place a kiss on her cheek, and hold her gaze. "Good morning. How are you today?"

"Good. I'm refreshed, had a good breakfast, and now I'm ready to see you at work."

"Okay then. Let's get out of here."

Whether Harleigh is interested in business or not, she looks keen to see what I do. That makes my heart melt, because not many women are interested in the logistics. It's usually the pound signs they're interested in. Well, that's the women that I used to attract. Maybe I have a guardian angel after all, and they've sent Harleigh to pick me up.

***

"It's a good location," says Samuel, the real estate agent.

I nod, look around, and watch Harleigh as she explores the building. If my memory serves me right, this was a bar-come-restaurant. A popular one at that. Most of the bars along the beach area are a big attraction for tourists, but to keep them coming back year after year, they need to serve amazing food and drink.

"Why is it for sale?"

"Owner is selling up and going back to England. Family issues. As you know, Gio, not many bars become available on the beach front. This will go quickly."

"When do you need an answer for?"

"Yesterday. Someone else is viewing it this afternoon. If you don't snap it up, my friend…" Samuel shrugs.

"Give me a moment." I walk over to Harleigh, who is out at the back door that looks out to the beach. People are sunbathing, kids are playing, and music is sounding from different locations. "What are you thinking, beautiful?"

Harleigh jumps, clearly carried away with the beauty in front of her. But when she turns to look at me, I can see the fear on her face. It isn't until she realises it's me that her features soften, and she relaxes. I could cause physical pain to her ex for ever hurting such a gentle soul.

"It's beautiful." She clears her throat. "Extremely busy. A good hotspot. What's not to like? I'm not business-minded, but it seems like it's a good opportunity."

I nod, place my hand on her hip, and look out to the dazzling blue sea. If I wasn't sold on the property before, just seeing Harleigh's reaction to the place has convinced me that this could be the best business decision I could ever make.

"I'll take it. Stop by the hotel tonight with the paperwork and we'll get the deal taken care of." I turn back and walk towards Samuel.

"You sure?"

"Absolutely. It's a little goldmine."

"Indeed, it is, my friend. Indeed, it is. I'll give you a call before I come by. Have a great afternoon."

I hold my hand out for Harleigh and she takes it. "I believe I owe you lunch for helping me make this decision."

"I did nothing." She giggles. "I just told you what I thought, which wasn't a business thought. But you can feed me. I won't turn down food. What do you suggest?"

"What do you fancy?"

"Something with chips. Don't ask where that came from."

"I know just the place. It's called the Hawaii Restaurant. It's one of the best places in Sunny Beach. The food is amazing, and it's just along here."

"Sounds good. So, what do you plan on doing with your new venture?"

"This might sound silly, so don't laugh."

"I'd never laugh at your ideas." Harleigh holds her hand up in Scouts' honour.

"Well, I've noticed that gin is a big hit back home just now, but over here, bars only really sell Gordon's Gin, Bombay Sapphire, and the odd pink gin. I want to focus on selling different kinds of gin. Of course, I'll have other things to sell, but gin would be the big thing. I'd also do food and hopefully appeal to a wide variety of customers."

"I love gin. Especially the flavours. I think you've hit the jackpot. Gin-ology." Harleigh shrugs off her name suggestion and I stare at her with curiosity. She must feel my eyes on her and turns back to face me. "Have I got something on me?" She looks down at her body.

I shake my head. "No. I love what you just said. I'm going to call the bar Gin-ology."

"Really? I was just sounding off."

"Really. You've just solved a huge problem for me, because Lucca and I would have fought over a name. Now, since Lucca seems to love you like a sister, I can say, 'Harleigh picked the name.'"

"No. No. No." She waves her hands in front of me. "I'm not getting stuck in the middle of you two. Nope." She laughs and looks around to see if anyone just witnessed her mini outburst.

I stop us and turn her to face me. I cup her cheeks with my hands and lean in to brush her lips with mine. The electricity is zapping through me already.

"There will be no fight in it now you've picked it. I love it."

I can feel the heat radiate from Harleigh's cheeks through to the palms of my hands. I like that she's so easy to get hot and bothered, but I wish I didn't know why compliments caused such a reaction. I'd rather my compliments didn't remind her of her past.

"What are you thinking about, Harleigh? I can hear the clogs turning."

She shrugs and smiles warmly. "This…" She points between us. "It isn't me. I don't even think I know what I'm doing. It's been so long since I liked a man or did anything like we're doing now."

Her flustered tone breaks my heart. I don't want to upset her or make her feel uncomfortable.

"We're having fun, Harleigh. Do you want to know what I think?" She nods and looks at my lips with delicate doe eyes. "I think you're over-thinking things. What we have going on between us is beautiful. I know how confusing these feelings are because I've never felt them before. But why waste time trying to analyse everything? We're in a beautiful country, enjoying each other's company. We're adults, and *if* something should blossom between us, I think we're big enough to deal with it. So, what do you say we just go for lunch and have a good time? Whatever happens after that, happens."

"Okay. I…" She lifts her eyes to look at me. "I think that's a good idea, Gio. I don't want to complicate things, but I don't want to push you away either."

"Good, because neither do I. This is just the beginning, beautiful."

I lean in and capture her lips with mine. The heat between us is scorching. How we're going to get through a lunch date without tearing each other's clothes off, I don't know.

I am going to need a lot of Dutch courage and restraint.

Chapter 10

Harleigh

Giovani parks his car outside his house and we get out slowly. It's as if everything we've done and said today is finally hitting us. We've both admitted that we feel something for one another. We've both admitted that these feelings are something we've never felt before. Even before my last relationship turned sour, I never felt butterflies in my stomach, or felt thrilled about a relationship. I went along with relationships because my friends were doing it. I've never jumped in headfirst because I wanted to, because I had strong feelings. I guess you could say that peer pressure was a big thing for me. It's only the last twelve months that I've been free from toxic relationships and fake friends, and I'm now, for the first time, looking forward to starting again.

I take in a deep breath and exhale slowly. I don't know what Giovani and I have going on between us, but the butterflies are real. The feelings he invokes are consuming me; heart, body, and soul.

I look up at Giovani's house like it's the first time I've seen it. It always looks more and more beautiful with every glance. I should make my excuses to go back to my hotel, but Giovani is like a magnet to me. I can feel myself being drawn to him.

"Do you fancy coming in for a drink? Lucca will be at the hotel sorting the week's deliveries."

I nod. I should be shaking my head, but for the first time in my life, I don't want to be sensible. I don't want to listen to my head. I want to be impulsive and follow what my heart and body wants.

"A drink sounds good. This has got to be the hottest temperature I've been in for a long time."

"Thirty-seven degrees this afternoon. You can always cool off in the pool with me."

I've got my bikini under my clothes, but could I swim with Giovani? Would he think differently if he saw me half naked? My body is not model-like. It has scars, internally and externally. I have curves and imperfections. I'm not the put together woman Giovani sees in the beautiful clothes and make-up. Without it all, I'm just a regular plain Jane.

"What did I say about over-thinking things?"

I smile and shake my head. "I'm trying. I really am, Gio. You might need to be a little patient with me. Sometimes it's hard to shake away the voices."

"It's a good job I'm a very patient man, Harleigh. Come on, let's get cool." Gio holds out his hand to me.

I slide my much smaller hand into his and let him lead the way. At this precise moment, Gio could be leading me to the devil himself, but I wouldn't care as long as he was there with me.

"Live a little, doll. You deserve it," echoes in my ears from my brothers back home.

We walk into Gio's kitchen and I kick off my shoes. The cold ceramic tiles against my hot, sticky feet feels amazing. I moan in satisfaction and I can't stop it.

"You have an amazing floor. I could lie on it." I fan myself with my hat.

"I'm pretty sure that could be arranged." Gio hands me an ice-cold bottle of water, but pulls it back as I reach for it and leans it against my neck. I sag with relief. The cold bottle is better than anything I've ever felt.

"Let me go and get swimming shorts on and I'll show you the delights the pool has to offer."

I take the bottle from Gio and watch him walk away from me like an Adonis. His muscular frame stretches the material of his shorts and shirt.

I give myself a fan and slide open the patio doors that lead out to the back garden. The pool does look inviting, I'll give him that. I put my bottle of water on the table and walk over to dip my toes in the water. I sit down on the edge of the pool. The cold water sends me into a trance. At this moment, I don't care who sees me sitting here soaking up the sun. My body is craving the coolness more than my self-conscious mind needs privacy.

"I've brought out some water-resistant sunscreen. I don't want that beautiful skin of yours burning." I jump as Gio comes up behind me, because I was carried away with the coolness on my skin rather than concentrating on my surroundings.

He throws down towels on the lounger. He kneels behind me, moves my hair to the side, and massages cold cream onto my bare shoulders. It sends my whole body into a tailspin. I've never felt so cared for, apart from my family, but you expect that from your family. This is a good feeling. A feeling I didn't think I'd crave as much if it came along. Who am I kidding? I never thought I'd come across a man so kind and caring.

"That feels so good," I moan.

"Good."

He stops massaging my back, shoulders, and arms a little too quickly for my liking. I could sit here and let my front fry with the sun if it meant Gio kept doing what he did. I'm glad I put this play suit on today, because the back is pretty bare with thin spaghetti straps. It gives him perfect access to my back and shoulders without me needing to take it off.

I look over my shoulder to see what Gio's doing, but he jumps into the pool and surfaces, rubbing the water off his face and hair. I'm a little annoyed that I didn't get to ogle his body with no clothes on. My cheeks heat at the thought, and I look down to my hands linked together between my knees. Gio swims over to me, lifts my hands out from between my legs and runs his fingers through mine.

"Don't over-think things, remember. Why don't you join me?"

I look down at my suit and stall. Eurgh! I want to join him, I do. I just wish I had more confidence to dive in headfirst.

"You can come in with your suit on if you like. I'm sure I can find a t-shirt and shorts to fit you after we get out."

I like how Gio seems to read my mind. It saves me going into embarrassing conversations. I take in a deep breath and imagine myself pulling up my big girl panties. I stand up from the side and let my suit fall to my feet. I pick it up and throw it over to the lounger. I slide into the cold water and gasp as every nerve ending tingles and protests the cold water, but it's an invigorating feeling. I feel amazing.

"Better?" Gio asks.

"Yeah. I could get used to this. I haven't spent any time in the pool since I arrived, and usually that's the first place I visit first."

"Well, feel free to come and use my pool anytime you like. The pool at the hotel doesn't get too crowded, but if you're looking for an escape then it can be a bit much."

"Thanks. Do you spend a lot of time in the pool?"

He swims farther away from me on his back. "I swim every morning if the weather is decent. There's something very invigorating about a swim in a cold pool to start your day."

"Yeah, I guess you're right."

I swim out to the middle of the pool to be beside Gio. He sits up from his back quickly and wraps his arm around my waist to draw me to him.

"I've wanted to do this all day. In fact, if I'm being honest, I've wanted to do this since the first moment I saw you. Something about you called to my heart and soul."

"Ditto. But I'm not particularly good at things like this."

"Said who?"

"You just lie there like a sack of potatoes. You're absolutely no use in the bedroom. I don't know why I put up with your Virgin Mary attitude."

I look into Gio's eyes, take charge, wrap my legs around his waist, and pull myself as close to his body as I can. "It doesn't matter. It was a nobody. I need to stop living in the past."

"And right here, we're very much in the present. Just two adults, living their best life, enjoying each other's company.

Nothing needs to go any further. We take this at your own pace, even if that means we spend your full holiday visiting sights, drinking alcohol, and swimming in my pool."

I take the lead for the first time in my life, lean in, and capture Giovani's lips with mine. It's soft and careful, empowering and life-changing, because no other kiss will ever compare to this.

His hands wrap in my hair and tilt my head to give him better access. Thankfully, the water is keeping me in place because I've been rendered powerless. The passion, the heat, and the tenderness are enough to leave me soaring high.

Gio pulls back from me and our foreheads lean against one another's. His hands caress from my neck, down to my shoulders and back, finishing on my hips to hold me in place.

"Do you see what you do to me, Harleigh?"

I can feel his erection pushing against his shorts, probing my centre. I'm seeing stars just from the contact and kiss.

"You have amazing hands," I blurt out.

It's only when the words leave my mouth that I hear how absurd they are and start giggling.

"I'm pretty sure my hands could be great at many things."

He pulls the ties at the side of my bikini bottoms and it falls off me. I feel him even closer than before and I unashamedly push closer to him, rocking back and forth, making my body sing from the contact.

"You just tell me when to stop and I will. Okay?"

"Okay," I breathe.

I don't want him to stop. I want to know what I've been missing out on my whole adult life.

Gio walks us back to the edge of the pool and my back hits the wall. His hand roams down my stomach and finds my entrance. My swollen nub is calling out to be played with, teased, and tantalised. I lean my head back and let every feeling surface. The feeling is too much, but I can't get enough. I want to feel it all. He rubs my nub softly, pushes two fingers inside me, and circles his wrist expertly. I see stars. My body soars higher and higher until I'm calling out his name. My head falls forward and rests on Gio's shoulder. My heart is pounding. How could he make me come so quickly? I've never had an orgasm at a man's hand. Any man I've been with has been selfish in the bedroom department. It was all about them, their pleasure and feelings. I never once felt like I do now.

"I like that just orgasmed look on you; rosy cheeks, wild hair, and sparkling eyes. We should keep this look on you, Miss Harrison."

"I think I'd like that," I whisper.

I lift my head from Gio's shoulder confidently and run my thumb across his lips. "I want you, Giovani. Don't stop now."

"Are you sure?"

"I've never been as sure of anything my whole life. I'm sure."

I feel him wiggle down his shorts and his large member springs free and hits my stomach. The thought of him fitting inside me turns me on more.

"Are you on birth control?"

I'm glad someone is thinking clearly, because being safe never entered my head.

"I am. I'm clean. I was tested after…" I pause and blink away a memory because I don't want to ruin this moment. "I've not been with anyone since."

"I'm clean, too. But we can get out and…"

I lean in and capture his mouth with mine. Our tongues duelling, probing, exploring every crevice. "I trust you, Giovani."

He lines himself up with my entrance and pushes into me slowly. I feel full, fit for bursting, but it's only making my body climb higher again. I've had orgasms by my own hand, but this is something else.

I'm in cold water, but I can feel a sheen of sweat on my body as we both climb higher and higher. Gio strokes my clit every time he pulls out, making me delirious.

"Come with me, beautiful."

And that's exactly what I do. I call out, just as Gio's hands grip my back and draw me closer to him. My chest is squashed in between us, rising and falling from the rapid breathing. It's probably the most exercise I've had in years.

"That was amazing, Harleigh. Thank you for trusting me enough to share this moment with you."

"Thank you for treating me so special. I…" I trail off and look away from Giovani as tears threaten to fall.

"What were you going to say?" He uses his thumb to make me look at him. "You can tell me anything, honey. I want to know all there is to know about you."

I take in a deep breath and try to steady my breathing. "I was going to say I didn't know it could feel so good."

"With me, it will always be so good. You should be treated like a princess, worshipped, and cared for."

"Thank you."

"What do you say to a nice hot shower, some food, and we take a trip down to the harbour for a couple of drinks? I can show you another part of Nessebar, where you can shop until you drop."

"That sounds amazing. But, just to warn you, I don't think it will take much to make me drop now."

"When you get tired, just let me know and we can always come back here, or I can take you to the hotel. Your choice. Everything will always be your choice with me, Harleigh."

"I don't know what I did to deserve meeting you, Giovani, but I'm glad I did. Remind me to thank my brother for sending me out here."

"I think we can both thank your brother for sending you out here. My angel. My princess."

He leans in and captures my mouth once more. I'm afraid if he doesn't stop, we'll never get out of this house again. I'd quite happily spend the rest of this holiday in Giovani's arms.

Chapter 11

Giovani

Sitting beside Harleigh, looking out to the sunset over the harbour is a beautiful moment. One I'll never forget. I haven't had a chance to take advantage of a moment like this in such a long time. It has always been work, work, and more work. I haven't had someone in my life that's made me want to take time for me... until Harleigh walked into my hotel. I don't know what it is about this woman. She's gotten under my skin and hypnotised me. I should be saying it terrifies me, but I kind of like it. It's invigorating and exciting. A pretty little package all rolled into one.

For years, I've worn a happy mask to hide my true self. On the inside, I've felt hurt and betrayed, but on the outside, I've appeared to be a normal, happy guy. I've hidden the truth, even from my family. I licked my wounds silently, and looking back, it didn't do me any good, but it did push me into building this empire I have. The only thing is, an empire and money means nothing if you don't have anyone to share it with.

"It's a beautiful sight out here." Harleigh's soft voice breaks through my thoughts.

"It is, huh?" I look at her and twirl a long strand of hair around my finger.

I'm not admiring the sunset, I'm admiring the beautiful woman sitting beside me. Her golden skin is glowing brightly, just like the angel I believe she is. She looks radiant. In just a short space of time, she has grown in confidence and relaxed around me, even if she doesn't see it herself.

Harleigh turns to look at me, her head tilting into my hand.

"I was talking about the sunset, Gio."

"That's beautiful too, but nothing compared to you." I wink at her.

"Are you always so smooth and kind?" She turns in her seat and our knees knock into one another.

I shrug. "I'm Italian. I'm meant to be kind and gentleman-like. My mum would put me over her knee and spank my arse if I was any other way to a woman, and that would probably be after my dad knocked seven bells out of me. So, I guess you could say that what you see is what you get."

"Good to know. Remind me to thank your parents if I ever see them."

"They always joke that I was the son they raised right, and that Lucca is the wayward child. Streetwise. Wild. Nothing like my parents at all."

Harleigh laughs and my dick stirs to life. How can one sound be so sexual? "I can't imagine Lucca being anything like you. You're like yin and yang, black and white. You complement each other, but you're so different."

"You're right. He's like my right-hand guy. I can't imagine life without him. It would be very…" I think about the right word. "Quiet, boring, or just no fun at all."

"What does he work as? Or is he out here with you permanently?"

"Lucca has a degree in business management, but he's not really interested in using it properly. Hence why he's out here, investing in my projects and keeping out of my mum and dad's way. He's got a good eye for detail and business, but it's too boring for him. I keep him busy with odd jobs around the hotel. He fills in when I can't. He's like my second in command. All my workers see him as their boss, too. He just won't make it official. It's like he has this commitment phobia." I shrug.

I wish Lucca would see himself like I do. Like everyone he meets does – the strong-willed, fierce protector. The man that would protect anyone from harm.

"One day he'll settle down. I wish I could be as carefree as him. He's a free spirit. That's a unique quality to have in this day and age."

"You could be right there. It must be good to go to bed and wake up with no cares."

"Exactly. That's definitely one way to look at it."

Harleigh's phone rings in her bag and she leans down to get it. She frowns at her phone and answers it.

"Hello…"

I watch her carefully, but there's a heaviness on her shoulders that wasn't there a few moments before.

"Unknown number and no one speaks." She holds the phone out as if she's studying it.

"Maybe a wrong number."

"Maybe." She tosses the phone back into her bag. "I've had a lovely day, Gio. I…" She shakes her head and bunches up her shoulders. "I never imagined any of today to happen, but I'm glad it did."

"Me too. What about that shopping I suggested?"

"Can we do that another night? I'm exhausted. I don't think my feet will carry me much farther."

"Of course. We have plenty of time. Do you want me to walk you back to the hotel, or would you like to come back to my house?"

"The hotel, please."

"Okay." I feel deflated that she doesn't want to come to my house, but she puts her hand over my arm and stops me from standing.

"I only said the hotel because I don't want to make Lucca feel uncomfortable. It's his house, too. In the hotel, it's only me. I don't need to take other people's thoughts into account."

I nod. I don't know why the thought of leaving her at the hotel alone hurt me. I don't want to spend a moment away from her. I'd quite happily spend the rest of her holiday in her company.

"Okay then. Let's get out of here."

I throw down the money on the plate with the bill and hold out my hand for Harleigh's. Her small, delicate fingers entwine with mine. The electricity ignites and sparks through us. I've never felt that connection before, but now I have, I'm not sure I want to let that go.

Since Harleigh walked into my life, time seems to be against us. She's on holiday. Her life is in Scotland. She'll return to her life and I'll return to my daily routine here. The thought of that sounds boring.

The thought of being here without her is daunting. Having her around feels natural. Nothing is strained or awkward. It's like we're connected in every way. It's like I've known her my whole life. Being with Harleigh is as easy as breathing.

Chapter 12

Harleigh

Lying with my head on Gio's naked chest is soothing to my soul. I'm calm, relaxed, and in a little bubble of my own. I feel paralysed, in a good way. A contentment rushes over me that I've never felt before.

Gio's fingers running up and down my spine sends tingles to all the right places. It's weird, because I've never been into sex before. I've never felt like I could voice my opinions on what I liked or disliked, but with Gio, it's different. My libido has been awakened and I'm happy to experiment with things I've never tried before. It makes a difference because sex was always a chore, but now it's a need I'm happy to explore. To feel what it's like to be loved and cherished by a man is a power of its own. It's a consuming feeling the takes over my whole body. It's like an addiction, but one I don't mind being addicted to.

Even half asleep, Gio can make me feel cared for. It's an unusual feeling for me, but one I could certainly get used to. I didn't know that this was how it was supposed to be between a man and woman. I've read so many books with a happy ever after, but I thought that's where the stories ended, on the pages of a book. It's nice to know that men like Giovani really do exist, and women can be treated like a queen.

"Feeling your soft body leaning against me feels like I'm in heaven," whispers Gio.

"You're nice and warm, and firm, and comfortable," I ramble. "I could sleep for a week."

"Try not to sleep for a week, because it will waste our time together, but please do fall asleep on me. It will be nice to fall asleep and wake up with you in my arms."

"Don't you need to get back to Lucca?" I tilt my head back to look at him.

"He is a grown-arsed man. I'm sure he can fend for himself for a wee while. Besides, I text him earlier and said I was with you. Stop worrying about everyone and just feel this moment."

He leans in and captures my mouth. My hand roams up his smooth chest and finishes on his cheek. His warm hands, muscular body, and minty breath send a jolt to every nerve ending in my body, and just like that, I'm fully awake. He turns me over quickly, and a small squeal leaves my lips. He leans over me, staring into my soul. I feel like I'm dreaming. This kind of thing doesn't happen to me usually.

"You don't have to answer me, but I'm going to ask a question."

I nod. I'm not sure if I'm ready for the question, but I feel like I owe it to myself and Gio to be honest.

"I noticed the scars across your shoulder blade and stomach when we were in the shower. Was that him?"

Tears spring to my eyes instantly. I was hoping Giovani hadn't noticed my scars, because then I wouldn't have to get into the mental pain they've left.

"The one on my stomach was a ruptured spleen. Martin said I fell down the stairs over the laundry I was carrying. Only, the real truth is that I was pushed down the stairs. I was lucky it was only my spleen that needed to be removed. It was one of the earlier incidents and I honestly thought he'd change. The scar on my shoulder blade was from his belt. I don't know much about that one, because I think I passed out after the first couple of whips. I managed to piece myself together without going to the hospital." I sniffle and wipe away the fallen tears.

Just repeating that story makes my body ache and tingle. It's like I can feel the pain in my shoulder from the belt.

"I'm so sorry, baby. I…" Gio pauses and rubs my cheek. "I wish I could wring his neck with my own bare hands."

"You and me both, but I don't want him to take anything away from tonight, Gio. I've learnt to live with the scars, and if you can see past them too…"

"Hey." Gio tilts my chin to look him in the eye. "I see nothing but the beautifully kind woman you are. Yes, I hate knowing you were hurt, and I loathe the fact that you've suffered to get where you are today, but I love the courage and determination you show."

"I wish I'd met you years ago," I admit truthfully, because with Giovani the truth comes easily.

"Me too, but we're here now, and I want you all over again." He peppers kisses down my neck, nibbles my shoulder, and cups my breasts in his hands. My back arches, pushing closer to his body. I've never been a touchy-feely kind of person, but with Gio I want it all.

"Take me, Gio. I need you, too."

And just like that, the latest conversation is forgotten about and our bodies are consumed by lust.

We've already made love twice since we arrived back from the harbour, but I can't get enough of him. Gio's awakened a sexual beast inside me and I doubt it will be tamed anytime soon.

Giovani nestles in between my thighs, lifts my leg onto his hip, and he pushes into me in one swift move. My ankle tightens on his arse, pulling him in closer. Every inch of him is inside of me. In and out, up and down, it feels glorious. Every part of me is screaming out in pleasure and excitement. I don't want this feeling to ever stop.

"I'm not going to last long, babe. You feel amazing."

"Don't stop, Gio. Oh, God."

My body shudders as another orgasm hits me. I'm seeing stars as he finishes and empties himself inside. He collapses on top of me. Our hearts beat wildly. Our breathing erratic. It's amazing what a connection between two people can create.

"Stay with me tonight, Gio."

He lifts his head off my chest, kisses the tip of my nose, and smiles. "I wasn't planning on going anywhere."

Those were the best words I've heard all day. No. That's a lie. Those were the best words I've heard all year.

***

I stir in bed and stretch out my aching muscles. On one hand, I feel like I've climbed a mountain because every part of me aches, but on the other hand, I feel sated and peaceful. I feel like I've slept for a month. My energy levels are the highest they've ever been.

Then reality hits me and I realise the bed is empty. I sit up quickly, pull the sheet around my naked breasts, and dread washes over me. Did Gio leave without saying goodbye? I climb out of bed, pull on my robe, and enter the bathroom. I quickly fix my hair, wash my hands and face, brush my teeth, and feel a little calmer. I walk through the bedroom and out into living area of my hotel room. I still and lean against the doorframe as I see Gio sitting on the veranda doing some work on his laptop. His sunglasses are pulled down his face. He's showered and changed his clothes; he looks like a god. I don't know why I'm surprised. He looks put together every time I see him. It's hard to believe by looking at him that he's faced his own heartache and misery.

"Good morning, beautiful."

I'm too carried away with my thoughts that I didn't see that Gio is looking at me.

"Morning." I clear my throat and walk out to the balcony. I feel shy again, and I don't know why, because Gio has seen every inch of me and never once said he doesn't like any part of what he saw, including the horrible scars. He's never made one derogatory comment to me the whole time we've been together. I know he isn't Martin, but it will take a long time for me to get that through my brain… if ever.

"You look surprised to see me."

I pull out a seat and sit down beside him. "I thought you had left when I woke up to an empty bed."

Gio pushes his laptop aside, leans over the table, and captures my chin with his thumb and forefinger. "I would never leave without saying goodbye. I got Lucca to drop me off some clothes and my laptop. I thought you needed some rest after our adventures yesterday."

I feel the heat in my cheeks rise. My chest feels like it's burning from embarrassment. I have this horrible trait where every bit of my skin from my chest to my forehead turns beetroot red when I get embarrassed.

"Lucca knows you stayed here?"

"He does. And, I believe his words were, 'I'm glad you two found each other. Maybe your broken hearts can be repaired after all.'"

I nod and try to look anywhere other than Gio's eyes, but his grip on my chin stops me from moving. His lips capture mine softly, making my heart stutter.

"You look radiant this morning."

"I think I have you to thank for that. Is that coffee I can smell?" I smell the air and inhale, cherishing it like it's my last breath.

"There's some freshly brewed inside, along with some pastries, fruit, yoghurt, and some toast. I got Arlena to bring us up a few bits. Sit tight and I'll bring it out."

Gio springs up and walks away swiftly. I sit back in the seat and let the sea breeze swirl around me. It's refreshing. I'm afraid going home is going to pale in comparison. I can see why Gio loves it here so much. If I had the means to live this life, I think I would... no questions asked.

Gio rolls out a cart and sits it to the side of me. He hands me a cup and I swear I snatch it like a child in a sweet shop.

"I can't function without coffee." I giggle.

"I thought as much." Gio sits back in his seat beside me.

"You can finish your work. I'm quite happy to sit here and admire the view," I say boldly, looking directly at Gio.

"Good to know, Miss Harrison, but I can work anytime. I'd much rather sit here, admire my own view, and eat some breakfast with you."

I sit forward, scoop some fruit salad into a bowl, and lick my thumb from the juice that splattered over my hand. I can feel Gio's eyes burning holes through me, but I continue to be provocative. I'm never usually so out there when it comes to sexual innuendos, but Gio unleashes a side of me I didn't know existed. I feel different around him. Confident. Brave. Powerful. Three things I never thought I'd say about myself.

"If you keep doing that, beautiful, I won't be held accountable for my actions."

"Hmm!" I stab a piece of fruit with the fork and pop it into my mouth. "Juicy."

In two point five seconds, Gio is out of his seat, clasping his hands on my cheeks and kissing me like it's his last. Our mouths duel ferociously, sending me on a high. How can one kiss be everything?

Gio pulls back, takes my hand, and drags me through the hotel room until we're out of sight of the veranda. Not that I'd care, because with the way that kiss was going, I wouldn't have stopped him out there. We would have been up on indecent exposure charges, if that's even a thing here in Bulgaria.

My back hits the wall and Gio lifts me into his arms. My legs wrap around his waist, drawing him as close to my core as possible. He tears at my robe and lets it fall open, the cool breeze of the air conditioning sets every nerve ending on high alert and I moan out my pleasure.

Gio's mouth wraps around my breast and bites down tightly. It's not painful, but I feel a gush of heat straight to my core.

"Oh, God! I need you now, Gio."

I pull at his belt and yank his zip and button open like a crazy person. I'm surprised at my own behaviour, but Gio seems happy with my lack of restraint.

Gio's dick springs free, hitting my bare stomach. He guides himself to my centre and rams himself home. We both call out our pleasure, every muscle tightening around one another. I'm glad Gio has my legs wrapped tightly around him, because I doubt I'd stand freely. I can't even think straight.

I wrap my fingers in his hair, hold on, and let him do all the work to make us reach new heights.

"I'm not going to hold on much longer, beautiful."

At the sound of Gio's husky, lust-filled voice, my body detonates quickly. All power in my body leaves me and Gio holds me tightly as he shudders around me, grunting out his pleasure. Thankfully, his senses are still alert, and he keeps us both upright.

"Jesus. I'm never going to get enough of you, Harleigh."

"That makes two of us." I breathe out heavily.

Giovani puts his hands on my cheeks then tangles my hair through his fingers. At this moment, I've never felt as free of my past. There is something about Giovani that puts my body at ease and makes me feel alive.

Giovani walks us both into the room with me still in his arms and his semi-half-mast erection still inside me. Usually, any guy I've been with before does the deed and leaves me where they dropped me. It's amazing to have a man who cares for my needs just as much as he cares about himself, if not more. Giovani has never once put his own needs before mine. Even at the height of his orgasm, he makes sure I get there first.

"As much as I could just crawl back into this bed with you, it would be a shame to waste such a glorious day. So, how about a shower and we organise a day of something you want to do."

"I've been here for a few days and not been to the beach. I've heard a lot about the golden sands, warm water, and beautiful scenes."

"The beach it is then."

Giovani crashes his lips down on mine and every thought I just had evaporates into thin air. My senses are consumed by him once again. This man has a habit of making me a speechless puddle of nothing with no control of my own body.

I'm pretty sure I'm never going to want to leave this hotel room.

Chapter 13

Giovani

Sitting on the beach is something I've never done in my time here in Bulgaria. I can see the beach from the harbour, smell the salty sea, but being on it was never my idea of fun. Now I'm here with Harleigh, I've got a sense of all the things I've missed out on during my darker period. You can't come to Bulgaria and not take advantage of the best feature of Sunny Beach – the golden sands. Yet, I've never followed my own advice, which seems crazy now that I think about it.

Harleigh's mobile rings in her bag. She sits up, and instantly the loss of her head on my thighs is noticeable. With the lack of contact, I feel like a part of me is missing. She fishes through her bag for the phone and I try to look anywhere other than at her.

"Hello?" Harleigh answers.

She pulls her phone away from her ear and looks at it carefully.

"Something wrong?" I sit forward more and place my hand over her hip.

"I keep getting these calls, but no one is ever there. Is there bad reception out here?"

I shrug and look at her phone. "Not really. If they're getting to call you, they should be able to speak to you."

"My brother has been calling okay. These calls are just getting on my nerves."

"Ignore it. Come back and get comfortable."

Harleigh tosses her phone back into her bag and leans her back into my chest this time, her head leaning on my shoulder. The feel of her warm skin touching my bare chest makes me want her all over again. I don't think I'll ever get enough of this woman.

"Do you do this often?" she asks me, tossing her hair over her shoulder, looking up to me with her glorious brown eyes.

I shake my head. "Never. I've never once sat on this beach like this. I'll never be able to look at the sand and sea again without imaging your beautiful face."

"I know what you mean. It's a good job we've got a couple of weeks left before my holiday ends."

"I plan on savouring every moment, worshipping every inch of you, and making this holiday absolutely unforgettable."

"Sounds good. I'm pretty sure my family will love hearing all about the adventure I've been on. I think I've been a little stuck in my own head lately. A shadow of myself. If this holiday is teaching me anything, it's that I can have fun and be me without thinking everyone is watching me, waiting for me to mess up."

I wrap my arms around her waist and kiss her neck tenderly. "I find it very hard to believe that you could ever mess up. And, those people you mention clearly don't deserve you in their life. Focus on the people who care about you and want to see you succeed."

"You're right. I'm beginning to see that now."

"Anyone that can come to a foreign country on their own is strong, independent, and capable of sticking up for themselves. Once you realise how strong you are, maybe you'll start to let your guard down and enjoy life better."

She turns in my arms onto her side, her leg resting over mine.

"It's like you can read me so well. I already see a big difference in myself, Giovani. Back home, just a week ago, I doubt you would have recognised me, or if you did, you'd probably never have glanced at me twice."

"I doubt that, beautiful. But, now you can look forward to new beginnings… a fresh start. Thinking positive works wonders for the mind."

"You believe that? I'd say it's the people that work wonders for your health and wellbeing. Getting to know you and Lucca has been good for me. It's brought me out of my shell."

"Good. But I hope I'm slightly higher up that ladder than my brother. If not, I'll have to make sure I blow your mind."

She giggles in my arms. "There is no contest. Lucca is like the goofy brother that you can't ignore."

"Tell me about it. You can walk away, but I'm left with the goofball."

We both laugh. "I say the same about my brothers. They mean well, but they drive me crazy, especially with me being the only girl."

"Lucca and I would be the same if we had sisters."

We return to silence as we look out across the sea. Boats are going by, kids are playing in the sea, people are laughing and joking. It's a typical holiday destination. Many different nationalities in one place. Water sports flying across the sea. Music playing from people's iPhone's or MP3 players. I like it. My cares have just disintegrated with the breeze flowing around us.

"Do you fancy a paddle?" asks Harleigh.

"Sounds good to me. It's getting a bit hot sitting here."

Harleigh stands up, puts her flip-flops in her bag, and dusts her legs down from the sand. "It must be hot if you're feeling it."

I fold up the blanket I brought and put it inside my backpack. I came prepared; I've watched too many people get severe burns from sitting directly on the hot sand. That wasn't happening to us. I don't want to sit in hospitals with anyone, never mind Harleigh. Her skin is too beautiful and delicate.

"I love the heat, but sometimes, especially at this time of year, it can become monotonous. Morning, afternoon, and evening are never below twenty-five degrees, and the heat is draining."

"I can imagine. Come on. Let's cool off, Mr…" Harleigh turns to me and studies me. "Mr what? It just dawned on me that I don't know your second name."

"Russi. My name is Giovani Russi."

"Nice. A typical Italian name." She turns away from me and walks towards the water.

I throw the bag over my shoulder and follow Harleigh down to the edge of the water. Harleigh throws her head back the moment the cold water hits her feet. I say cold, but it's not that cold at all. It feels like a lukewarm bath.

"This feels amazing."

I hold my hand out for her to take and we walk along the edge of the water all the way back to the harbour at Old Nessebar. The feel of the water on my feet, the sun on my skin, the breeze through my hair, it's like a magnitude of feelings sparking every nerve ending in my body.

"Do you like good food, circus and cabaret acts, and the perfect sunset setting?" I ask Harleigh, lifting our joined fingers to my lips.

"It sounds amazing. I can't say I've been to any. Well, I did visit the circus with my family when I was a child, but the last few years…" She pauses and looks out to the sea.

I can sense the sadness that has just set upon her at something she remembers from her past. I pull us to a stop and brush some fallen hair away from her face.

"What were you going to say?"

She looks up into my eyes. "My life hasn't been pretty, Gio. Everything I'm doing now, the places I've seen, the fun I've had, it's all a novelty to me. I spent the last few years of my life like a hermit, stuck at home, enduring the physical and mental abuse from my ex. I don't want you to feel sorry for me, because that's not what this holiday is about. One thing I love about being with you is that you don't look at me with pity, and you don't handle me with kid gloves on. You treat me like a real person."

"Okay. I'm glad I don't make you feel uncomfortable. Just know that I admire you. Everything you've faced. You've been to hell and back, but here you are, spending time with me, showing the world that you're capable of moving forward."

"I'm determined not to keep letting my past shadow over me. It's hard when I think about why I've missed out on so much, but I won't let it take the enjoyment out of this holiday. My past has taken too much of me already. I won't let it take over my future as well."

I nod. "Good. So, tonight, Khan's tent. Dress up as much as you like and we'll enjoy some a la carte food, singing, dancing, and entertainment. I'll get a taxi to pick us up at seven p.m."

"Sounds fabulous."

I lean in and capture her lips softly. I'm afraid if I take it any deeper, we'll end up arrested for indecent behaviour on a family beach, and I don't want to waste one moment with Harleigh.

***

"Where have you been?" Lucca walks into the house and throws his keys down. "Where are you off to all dressed up?"

I smile and shake my head at my impatient brother. If he'd stop throwing question after question at me, I'd be able to get a word in.

"I was at the beach with Harleigh, and I'm taking her to Khan's tent tonight. You're more than welcome to join us."

Lucca pulls a bottle of water out of the fridge and glugs it down quickly. "I said I'd cover Karmen's shift behind the bar tonight, because she has a family gathering."

"Why didn't you say? I would have covered it and made plans for another night."

"I forgot. I agreed to it earlier in the week. It's no big deal. Besides, you and Harleigh deserve some time together. I take it things are going well if you didn't come home last night."

I feel the biggest grin appear on my face. I don't want to look smug, but just thinking about the time I spent with Harleigh is amazing. My body remembers every moan, every touch, and every scent associated with last night and this morning. I've never in my life spent the night with a woman and felt so captivated.

"It was good. Thanks for dropping stuff off for me this morning. I didn't want my hotel guests to see me in yesterday's clothes."

"No worries, bro. You've saved my arse plenty of times. So, Khan's tent, huh? You really like her?"

I nod. Admitting my feelings for Harleigh is invigorating. I can't lie and say it's just a bit of fun.

"I do. It's weird though, because we've only just met. She's only here on holiday. Who knows what's in store for us?"

"I'm only going to say this once, Gio. If she's the one, you need to hold on with both hands, make it work, and never let her go. Good women don't exist much nowadays."

"We'll see what happens. Oh, and before I forget, Harleigh named the new bar."

Lucca's eyebrows raise wildly. "And... Don't keep me waiting. Tell me already."

"She said it during a conversation we were having, and it really struck a chord within me."

"Fuck sake, just tell me." Lucca holds his hands up. He has never been big on patience.

"Gin-ology. It can be a gin bar by night, selling the most amazing brands of gin, something Bulgaria doesn't have. And by day, we can be a family friendly restaurant, selling cocktails and the best British foods we can. We can also think about having a sandwich and snack bar beachside."

"Sounds good. We can talk about it tomorrow afternoon in the office. We can get some graphic work started. I'll be in the hotel tonight when you get back. You and Harleigh come and have a drink with me."

"Will do. Call if you need me for anything."

"Just go and have some fun. Nothing much is going to happen, apart from families drinking, singing on the karaoke, and probably a lot of fun and laughter. I do actually like working the bar, ye know."

I pick up my wallet and phone and stick them in my pocket. "You should work the bar more often; the guests love it when you do."

Lucca reminds me of Tom Cruise in *Cocktail* when he gets behind the bar. He's full of fun and frolics.

"Don't push your luck, Gio. Go. Have some fun, before I change my mind and make you work."

"Right." I practically run out of my house, because as much as it's my business, the thought of leaving Harleigh alone tonight isn't sitting well in the pit of my stomach. In fact, living without Harleigh at all isn't sitting well with me, but that's a subject to digest another day.

Chapter 14

Harleigh

I've dressed to impress tonight. I was determined to look pretty and feel good in myself. I've forgone wearing make-up my entire trip so far, just because I've become used to wearing none, but tonight, I've dolled up to the nines, because I want to. In the pit of my stomach, I doubt my decision already. Maybe I should have just gone casual, let Gio see me the way he has every day so far. Maybe he doesn't like a woman caked in make-up. Maybe I'll just embarrass him.

"You look like a drag queen or a clown. Get that shit off your face," says Martin.

"Martin, it's only a bit of foundation and lip gloss."

"Don't answer me back, Harleigh. Just do as you're told for once. I am in no mood for your attitude tonight."

Martin storms out of the room and leaves me looking at my reflection in the mirror. I bang down my hands on my vanity table and the tears fall down my cheeks. I've never been big into make-up. I've always gone for the subtle look, but Martin hates anything I do. I just can't win. I take out the make-up remover wipes and scrub my face until I feel like I'm scrubbing the skin off. Maybe a red blotchy face will serve him right.

I sigh dramatically and flop down on my bed. I look at my watch and it says 6.50 p.m. Gio has had impeccable time-keeping skills so far. He won't be late tonight. It gives me ten minutes to give myself a shake, pull up my big girl panties, and prepare to have some fun.

I pick up my phone and speed dial my brother. It doesn't even ring twice before he answers.

"Harls, are you okay?"

I hate how whenever I call my family, the first thing they think is that there's something wrong with me. I know I've never given them much cause to think otherwise, but it still annoys me.

"Hello to you too. I'm fine. I just need you to talk me off the ledge." I hold my elbows on my knees and take a few deep breaths.

"What ledge? What's going on, Harls?"

I take in a deep breath, sit up straight, and close my eyes. "I've met someone. He's lovely. In fact, he's perfect, Gav. I just don't know what I'm doing. I'm so far out of my depth I'm drowning."

"Okay... I'm not seeing the problem, doll. You might have to break it down for me, but first take a few deep breaths and calm down."

I take in a few deep breaths and slowly exhale. I feel my heart rate lowering and my breathing regulate to a normal pace.

"There isn't a problem, it's me. He's taking me out to dinner tonight. I love spending time with him. He seems to enjoy spending time with me. He's a gentleman, Gavin." I sigh.

Even sitting here listening to myself I can hear how stupid I'm being. My lack of confidence in myself and other people has its downside. It's like having a devil on one shoulder and an angel on the other, only the devil usually kicks the angel to the kerb and allows me to spiral out of control. Usually, I bury myself in work at that point or hide away with a bottle of wine and a box set. Here, there's nowhere for me to run and hide.

"Unless there is a big but coming along, I'm not following why there's a problem."

"It's just me."

"Listen to me, Harls. Anyone who has you in their life should be bloody honoured. You're the most amazing person I've ever met. You like this guy, right?"

I nod. "I do. I've never felt this way before. I know it's stupid, It's a holiday fling, but..."

"But nothing. You're young, free, and single. Live your life to the full. It's about time you start living, Harleigh."

A knock sounds on my door and I jump up, startled. I feel like a naughty teenager about to be caught doing something they shouldn't be.

"He's here, Gav. Oh my God."

"Good. Stay calm and just enjoy yourself. Send me a picture of you both. I'm good at judging a book by its cover."

I growl at my brother playfully. I know he's being serious though. That's why I'm not taking him on. "Okay. I'm going. Thank you for listening to me be a paranoid wreck."

"Anytime. And for what it's worth, I'm glad you're having fun."

"All thanks to you, Gavin."

"I won't tell you I told you so. I'm hanging up. Go and have fun."

And he hangs up the phone without a goodbye. I smile at my brother, toss my phone down on the bed, and walk slowly to the door. I've taken so long to answer it, I wouldn't blame Giovani if he left. But he's leaning against my door frame with a bunch of flowers in his hands.

"I thought you had stood me up." Giovani smiles brightly and hands me the flowers.

It's then that I notice that he's dressed in black trousers, a white short-sleeve shirt open at the top of his chest, and dress shoes. He looks delicious.

"I was on a call to my brother, Gavin."

He follows me into the hotel room. I fill up the sink with water and place the flowers in it. They're gorgeous and they brighten up my room. No, they brighten up my mood. No man has ever bought me flowers before.

"I'll get a vase sent to your room for them."

I turn back to face him, taking in a deep breath. My heart is racing again, my palms are sweaty, and my legs feel shaky.

"Wow! You look amazing."

"Really? I was just having a moment. But my brother told me to go have fun. If he could have pushed me out the door himself, I'm sure he would have."

Gio walks towards me and rests his hands on my hips. "I like the sound of your brother."

"Hmm! I bet you two would get along like a house on fire."

"I don't want anything burning, unless it's your panties."

I giggle. "You're terrible."

Gio leans in and kisses me tenderly. I feel every nerve in my body standing to attention, but this time for a totally different reason. You wouldn't think that ten minutes ago I was close to a panic attack. Yet, a few moments in the arms of Giovani, and my heartbeat is racing for a whole other reason. The goosebumps are rising on my skin and my body feels like a pile of mush, but not because I feel weak. No. I feel powerful and on top of the world.

"I think we should go to dinner before I end up stripping you out of this delectable dress and having my wicked way with you right here in this lounge."

"Promises," I tease and walk on wobbly legs to collect my bag. "Before you carry out your threat, I think we should get out of here because I've been neglecting my stomach this afternoon. Not that it will do me any harm."

Gio captures me around the waist and draws me back to his chest. "It will indeed do you harm. I happen to love your body the way it is. You're stunning, Harleigh. I'll spend every day of your holiday showing you - telling you - just how beautiful you are."

I can feel the smile on my face as wide as it ever has been. Nothing and no one has ever made me smile the way Giovani does. I wish I could bottle him up and take him home with me. Have my own little dose of Giovani whenever I want.

He twirls me out of his arms - I'm glad I've got flat sandals on - and he takes my hand in his. I grab my bag and we walk out of my room like a couple on holiday would. Only, what are we? A holiday romance? Friends with benefits? Fuck buddies? Eurgh...why do things need to have a label? It only confuses things more.

We make our way down to the lobby in no time at all. Lucca is walking in through the main double doors, dressed in black trousers and a pink shirt rolled up at the sleeves. He looks different to the carefree man I've come to know. I don't think I've seen him in anything other than shorts and a vest.

"Is Lucca coming with us?" I ask, trying to remove my hand from his, but he holds on tighter.

"No. He's working the bar tonight. I said we'd come in for a drink on our way back."

"Remember me when you're eating, drinking, and having fun. Remember I'm the party brother, Harls," Lucca calls over his shoulder as he passes by and heads towards the bar.

I can't help but laugh at him. I know from working with kids that egging him on by laughing is the worst thing I can do. Lucca is just like a doe-eyed child. The boisterous child in the class that likes to get up to mischief. That thought makes me smile.

Gio walks towards a black car and pulls open the door. "Sorry, Giovani. I was taking a business call." A man jumps out of the driver's seat.

"No worries. Rio, this is Harleigh. Harleigh, this is Rio, our driver for tonight. He runs this taxi company."

"Nice to meet you, Rio."

"Likewise, Miss Harleigh." He runs around the car and holds his hand out to me. "I hope you have a good evening."

I shake Rio's hand and climb into the well-maintained car. It's comfortable and cool, nothing that I expect from a local taxi. This is luxury at its finest.

One thing I've picked up from Bulgarians is the respect they show to tourists. I've not come across a horrible person yet. Back home in Scotland people wouldn't spit on you if you were on fire, especially if it didn't have any gain for them. It isn't until you come to foreign countries that you see the stark contrast. It upsets me, because Scotland is a lovely part of the world. The people leave a lot to be desired

We set off and I look out of the window, taking in the sights Bulgaria has to offer. People are milling around in their beach attire, laughing and joking. I've not really had a chance to get to know anyone else in Bulgaria. Once I met Gio and Lucca, anything I planned to do was forgotten about. Now, I'm quite happy to be chauffeured around and shown all the best places. I wouldn't have done half of what I've done so far if I was on my own.

"You'll love Khan's tent. My mum and dad go every time they come out here. It never gets boring."

"It sounds…." I pause and think about the best word. "Interesting." I turn my attention to Gio and our knees brush, sending sparks straight to my core. "When was the last time your parents were out here?"

"Last year. They're due their yearly visit, but they just turn up and surprise us. At first, when I didn't have the house, I was never organised, and by luck, I always had a room spare in the hotel they could use. Now, with the house just around the corner, they can stay with me if they so desire, much to Lucca's annoyance. He'd much rather I flung them in the hotel and forgot about them for their entire stay."

"Lucca and your dad really don't get along, huh?"

"They're just so alike, but neither of them would admit that. I keep hoping that one day Lucca will settle down, find the one, have kids, and then realise my dad isn't as bad as he thinks. Lucca just sees Dad as a nag, trying to control his life. And I'm not condoning what my dad is like around Lucca, because it's wrong, but I see both of their sides. My mum just sits back and watches the fireworks, because she's old school and doesn't interfere with anything her husband says. It annoys Lucca, because he thinks Dad takes the piss because Mum is so laidback."

"Let's hope the right woman comes along one day and sets Lucca on the right path."

"I'm not going to hold my breath on that one, sweetheart. Lucca is a free spirit."

I look out of the window beside Gio and notice we're climbing up a hill. The hustle and bustle of Sunny Beach has faded. It's like another world… again. Every time I think nothing else will surprise me here, something comes along and changes my mind. Each thing I see is more beautiful than the last.

"I bet you wonder where on Earth I'm taking you now."

"Just a little. But I trust you. I'm just enjoying the ride." I smile.

I'm glad my face is caked in make-up to hide the blush that's usually permanently stuck to my cheeks.

At that moment, we round a sharp bend and turn into what I assume is our destination.

"Enjoy the show, guys," says Rio, as he pulls up to the side.

I follow Gio out of the taxi and he takes my hand. I look up to the most beautiful building I've ever seen. It's actually set out like a tent, but it's built with brick instead of fabric.

"Wow! It's stunning."

It's breath taking. There isn't a word good enough I can use to describe it, it's that beautiful.

"Let me show you the magnificent view."

Gio pulls me along behind him and I follow willingly. The night air is still humid and warm. Other tourists are walking around the area, getting ready to go inside to settle down to dinner. The whole atmosphere is something else.

We climb a few steps and Gio pulls me over to the wall. I look out over the whole area of Sunny Beach, the sand and sea below us. The views are magnificent. It's like a scene from a postcard. It's every photographer's dream.

"It's even better at about nine o'clock when dusk is setting in. If we're not too carried away with the acts, I'll bring you back out."

I place both of my hands on the wall and throw my head back to take in a lungful of air. It's amazing what clean air can do, not just for your lungs, but for your wellbeing too. I've only been here a short time and my skin and hair are so much healthier. My mental health isn't on par just yet, but it's better than it was back home. Everything feels so much better here.

"I've said this a lot lately, but I could so get used to this."

"Me too."

I look over at Gio and he's staring right at me with a cheeky smile on his face. I don't want to be too forward and ask if he's talking about the same thing I am. My head and heart need to think that he means me, and not the sun, sea, and amazing views.

I take the proverbial bull by the horns, lean forward and kiss Gio a little harder than I planned. I'm relieved he doesn't mind public displays and openly kisses me back with no hurry.

I pull back and his forehead rests down on mine. I feel his warm breath against mine.

"Maybe we should go inside," I whisper against his lips.

He winks at me, takes my hand, and we walk slowly around the building, taking everything in. If what I've already seen is not the main thing then tonight is going to be a ten out of ten… and I don't just mean the man.

What is this man doing to me?

Chapter 15

Giovani

Sitting beside Harleigh, watching her clap and cheer for the trapeze acts flying through the air, is the best thing I've heard and seen in what feels like forever. Her hair is down, her body is relaxed, and she's enjoying herself. I'm glad I thought about bringing her to Khan's tent now. Anyone that comes up here and doesn't enjoy themselves needs a personality transplant. Kids from a young age, to grandmas at eighty-years old enjoy the atmosphere. The entertainment, the views, and the building alone are the main attractions. The food and drink are just a bonus.

"This is so much fun. Does it have to end?" Harleigh pouts and makes me smile at her innocence.

The lights come up and everyone cheers loudly. I can feel the applause vibrating through my body it's that loud.

"I'm afraid it does. Did you enjoy it?"

"Absolutely amazing. It's the best thing I've ever watched… ever."

I'm over the moon that Harleigh enjoyed this little beauty spot. I'd go as far as saying it's one of the best nights out in Bulgaria. People come from all over the world just to experience what Khan's tent has to offer. It's the one place I tell all my hotel guests that they must visit.

Harleigh drinks the last of her glass of wine. Her eyes are sparkling from the alcohol; a look I've started to like on her. It's the one time I get the true Harleigh. There's no filter, no thinking about what she needs to say or do. She's just pure and relaxed. I wish she didn't need alcohol to fuel that side of her, but I won't stop trying to break down her walls until I get this side of her all the time.

"Would you mind if I took a photo of us together? I promised my brother I'd take a picture, and it isn't something I'd usually do, but I'm trying out this new me. I have social media, but I've not used it for a long time. It just seems fitting that I take a picture of us tonight when we're all relaxed, dressed up, and having fun. It might show my brother that I got over my panic attack earlier and did actually have fun."

I reach over and take her hand.

"I just rambled, didn't I?" We both laugh. "It sounded okay in my head."

"You never need to ask to take a photo. Let's ask someone to take a full-length picture instead of a selfie."

I stand up and ask the gentleman from the next table, who is English, if he'll take a picture. He's only too happy to oblige.

Harleigh stands up beside me, looking happy and merry. She hands her phone over to the man and he snaps a picture of us.

"Thank you," we say in unison.

"One more." I take out my phone, turn the camera around and snap a closer picture of us together.

I show Harleigh the picture and she pats my chest. "Anyone looking at that picture would think we're a couple."

I look at the photo carefully as she grabs her bag. It's at that moment I don't doubt what she says. I want everyone to see me with Harleigh. I want the whole world to know she's mine. Only, I don't know what we are. We're enjoying each other's company, having the best sex I've ever had in my life, and somehow, we're riding the biggest wave of ecstasy.

"Ready?" Harleigh asks brightly.

I love the contagious glow she has about her tonight. Her smile that reaches her eyes. I'll remember this night for as long as I live.

"Sure. Let's get out of here. Rio will be waiting outside."

I find it hard to believe that I've only known Harleigh for a short time, because life seems so natural with her; eating drinking, spending time together… the only thing that feels wrong is being away from her.

Is that a sign that we're destined to be together? I don't believe in guardian angels, but someone is looking out for us.

Chapter 16

Harleigh

When we walk into the hotel, music is playing in the bar, and laughter and chatter surround us. The heat from Giovani's hand is making me hotter than the Sahara Desert. I have pools of sweat on my palms. Actually, I have sweat in places I didn't know I could have sweat.

"I've had such a lovely evening." I look over at Gio.

"Good. I'm glad. I did too. I'll have to up my game for our next date night."

My heart flutters in my chest at the thought of another night with Gio. He hasn't got fed up with me just yet, and that thought alone excites me. No man has ever just wanted to spend time with me without it being for their own gain. It's something I'll need to get used to, because it's a strange feeling. Foreign to me and my body. But I have to say, I like it. I like the feeling of being wanted. Needed.

"And you'll be happy to know my bar stocks gin, and plenty of it."

"Ah, that's finished my night off perfectly. I'm not a big drinker, but I do like to taste test a lot of the different flavours.

My brother brings me a different bottle back from every trip he takes. I have a funny collection back home."

I don't know what it is about Giovani, but I find it so easy to discuss things with him. I openly tell him about my life without even thinking about it. I've never done that before.

"I get a lot of British tourists staying here so I like to give them what they like back home," Giovani explains.

We walk into the bar and it's the busiest I've ever seen it.

"Karaoke is always busy."

I smile at Giovani, because it's like he read my mind. He seems to know what I'm thinking all the time. Either I'm easy to read, or he makes it his mission to be attentive.

It's good to see people enjoying themselves with their loved ones. I was beginning to think this hotel held the hoity toity upper class citizen, but who can avoid karaoke? No one. I know I'm the worst singer out there but give me a few drinks and a singing partner and I'll give it a go.

We spot a space at the bar and Gio pulls out a barstool for me. I hitch myself up, probably not ladylike, and sit patiently and wait for Lucca to spot us. He looks stressed and very unlike the guy I've come to know. What could have possibly happened since earlier this evening?

"Oh, shit," says Gio, and I look over to where he's looking in the corner.

A little elderly couple are sitting tapping their hands on the table, drinking their drink, enjoying the music.

"What's wrong?" I ask curiously.

"That's what has crawled up Lucca's arse tonight."

"What?"

"You wanted to meet my mum and dad, right?"

"Erm... Is that?" I point over to the corner.

"Give me two minutes, babe." He leans down and kisses me softly on the lips.

It was the quickest kiss we've ever shared. I don't like seeing Gio and Lucca worked up. It breaks my heart, because I've got used to their carefree nature.

I watch Giovani walk over to his parents. His mum spots him instantly and stands up to embrace her son. It's a lovely moment I'm glad I witnessed. Gio really cares about his mother; that much is obvious, even from a distance.

"He spotted them, then."

I look over at Lucca as he leans across the bar. He looks like the weight of the world is on his shoulders and I wish I could take some of the weight off.

"He did. Are you okay?" I reach over and squeeze his arm.

"Yeah. What can I get you to drink, Harls?"

"Gio said you have gin. Just give me any flavour with lemonade, and whatever Gio usually drinks here."

"Coming right up."

I really wish I could jump into Lucca's head and find out what his problem is with his parents. He looks terrible tonight, and I hate that look on him.

"Ice?"

Okay. So, we're down to one-word questions.

"Please. Plenty of it. I need to cool down."

Lucca places my drink down on the bar and a bottle of beer for Gio. I take out my purse and hand over the money, but Lucca just pushes my hand away.

"It's on the house. Enjoy."

"Thanks. Listen, do you fancy being my lunch buddy tomorrow? Maybe you can show me your idea of a good lunch. My treat, of course."

Lucca leans over the bar with a drink of his own in his hand. "Why not? What do you fancy?"

"Anything. Surprise me."

"McDonalds is out then." He winks at me.

"Hey, I like McDonalds." I laugh, just as a hand lands on my lower back.

I look up at Gio and smile warmly. "Hey."

"Hey. I've got some people who want to meet you if you're up to it?"

I look around Gio carefully and see a smiling man and woman looking at us carefully. It's like they're afraid to blink in case they miss anything.

"Okay," I say warily.

I'm not good with meeting strangers, but if they're anything like Gio and Lucca then I know they'll be absolutely fine. I hope.

"Good luck, Harls," Lucca calls over to me as he walks away to serve some customers, which just puts me on edge even more.

"Ignore him. Honestly, the only person who has an issue with our parents is Lucca." Gio lifts our drinks from the bar and carries them expertly in one hand while taking my hand in his. I'm glad of his hold on me because it gives me confidence.

"Harleigh, this is my mum, Margo, and my father, Alexandro."

I shyly hold out my hand to the elderly couple, but Margo walks straight up to me and wraps her arms around me. I feel huge in her small frame.

"Bella." She holds me out at arm's length and studies every part of me. "It's wonderful to see that someone beautiful has captured my son's heart and soul."

"Grazie." I say in the only Italian I know.

"Nice to meet you, my dear. Please, call me Alex." Alexandro holds his hand out to me and tenderly shakes mine.

It's easy to see where Gio gets his soft, tender touch from. In fact, Gio looks extremely like his father in every way. His eyes, hair, and face shape are all Alexandro.

"Come and have a drink with us." Margo points to their table and Gio puts down our drinks. He pulls out a seat for me and I gratefully accept it. When I'm behind a table, I can hide my insecurities and play with my hands, fidget with my dress. Anything if it contains my nerves.

Only that doesn't happen, because Gio reaches over and takes my hand and holds it tenderly between his. It's as if he heard my thoughts and tries to break my tradition. That wouldn't be a bad thing, because I hate my nerves and anxiety. I'd do anything to lose them.

"So, this is a nice surprise. What brings you out here?" asks Gio.

"We just wanted to see our sons. It has been a while, and it's clear you're not coming out to Italy any time soon." Margo reaches over and squeezes Gio's arm.

"We've just been so busy, Mum. We're opening a new bar soon; the paperwork and planning is taking up all of our time. We won't get home any time before the season ends."

"Here?" asks Alex.

"What?"

"The new bar. Is it here?"

"Sunny Beach. It's a good business decision. One we've seen coming for a while. When it did, Lucca and I jumped on it."

I hear the uncertainty in Giovani's voice. And for the first time since I've met him, I see a vulnerable side. I squeeze his hand and he gazes down at our joined hands and winks at me.

"And what about you, dear? Do you live out here?" asks Alex.

"I don't. This is just a holiday. I'm a teacher, first and foremost. I'm also a freelance editor in my spare time, but it's more of a hobby now, I love it so much, I couldn't give it up when I went into teaching fulltime."

"How did you meet?"

I feel like I'm on the spot and getting asked sixty questions. I just hope I don't fail this interrogation. I've never had to meet the parents before. Martin's mother died when he was a child and he didn't speak to his father and stepmother. This is new territory for me.

"Here, actually. We haven't known each other all that long."

"Ah, early days. That's the fun part," says Margo.

"It is. You've raised two lovely sons."

"We've tried." Alex sighs. "I'm not sure where we got Lucca from. Giovani makes up for them both."

I look over at the bar and Lucca is moping around. I feel this absurd need to stick up for him.

"I happen to think Lucca is amazing. He's been fantastic with me since I've been in Bulgaria. He works hard, he's kind, and he's fun to be around. He's a good friend. Loyal. And that's something extremely hard to come by nowadays."

"Are you sure you've picked the right brother?" asks Alex.

I choke on my own saliva. Did he just ask that question? I'm taken aback, but I find myself straightening my back. I look over at Gio and I'm hoping he sees my apology before I let go of my anger. I can't sit here and feel bullied by someone who doesn't know me. I vouched after Martin that I'd stick up for myself and the people I care about. That extends to Lucca and Gio now. They've showed me nothing but kindness and respect since I landed on their doorstep.

"There is no question in my mind that Gio is who I'm meant to be here with. However, I see Lucca as a friend. A good friend at that. I've had enough rubbish happen to me over the last couple of years and I happen to be an *extremely* good judge of character. Gio, I've had a lovely evening, but I think I need some beauty sleep."

"I'll walk you up to your room."

"No." I hold my hands up to him. "Please, stay and be with your parents. I'll speak to you tomorrow." I lean over and kiss his cheek. "It was nice to meet you, Mr and Mrs Russi."

I probably could have done better, but I'm angry. I feel the anger coursing through my veins so much that I could cry. I'm a terrible crier when I'm angry. It's a trait I picked up from my mum. I think I did well to remain true to myself. I got my point across and remained polite.

"Harleigh!" I hear behind me.

I look over my shoulder and see Lucca jogging after me. "Wait up. What happened back there?"

I shake my head. I didn't want to get Lucca involved in what just went down, because he has a big enough issue with his parents. It's clear to me that Margo isn't the issue. She's kind and accommodating. The perfect mother figure.

"Nothing. I'm just going to my room. I've had enough excitement for one day."

"Yeah, and I'm Santa Claus. Pull the other one, Harls. What happened when you met my parents?" he grinds out and carries on walking behind me into the lift.

"Nothing. They're..." I pause for the right word. "Charming. Are we still on for lunch tomorrow?"

"I'll let this go for tonight. I'll call you in the morning to arrange a time."

"Okay. Goodnight, Lucca." I reach over and squeeze his arm before leaving the lift on my floor.

I don't hang around any longer than I need to, because there is only so long that I can lie to Lucca. I hate lies, but I'd rather distort the truth as opposed to make him hate his family more. I won't have that on my conscience.

I pull out my key card and swipe it down my door. The moment it clicks open, I feel the stress lift from my shoulders. I'm in my own little cocoon. I'm away from questions, interrogations, and prying eyes. I hate being put on the spot, but I didn't expect Gio's dad to be so forward. If he's like that all the time, I can see why Lucca has a problem.

I throw down my bag, kick off my shoes, and throw myself down on my bed. I hate how I feel right now, because just two hours ago I was happy, enjoying my time with Gio, and dancing the night away. Now, it's like that dark cloud is hanging over me, just waiting to burst into a terrible storm.

I reach over for my bag, grab my phone, and set out to reinstall my Facebook and Instagram. I've been away from all social media for such a long time. Martin didn't like me having contact with the outside world. Even when I got away, it felt wrong to have social media when I didn't feel very social. Tonight, right now, I want to show the world that I was happy and enjoying life just a few hours ago. I'm not this hermit that people have come to expect from me.

The moment my accounts are reactivated, I upload the picture that was taken of Giovani and me just a short while ago. I caption it, *'Having the time of my life.'* I hit send before I can change my mind. I know I can delete it later, but I feel ten feet tall doing something that I haven't done in such a long time. It's crazy how such a mundane task can make me feel like a queen.

A moment later, my phone vibrates. I snatch it up off my stomach and open the notification. I smile when I see my brothers' comments. *'Welcome back to the wonderful world of Facebook, doll. Looking fabulous!'* wrote Gav.

'*Bulgaria obviously agrees with you, sis. Looking good,*' wrote Sebastian.

I smile, roll my eyes, and roll onto my stomach, holding up my weight on my elbows.

'Sun, sea and… shopping will do that to someone.' I write back quickly and giggle at the thought of their jaws dropping to the ground when they imagine what I was going to write back. I know this will be a novelty to them, because I haven't been much of a sister lately. I've been a shell of myself. I've worried my family, sent them to hell and back, and now I'm at the opposite side of the world. But knowing they're happy because I'm enjoying myself is rewarding, as crazy as that sounds.

I sigh, place my phone on the bedside table, and roll out of the bed. A shower, clean pyjamas, and a good sleep should help me forget the last half an hour tonight. Because whatever happens, none of it was Giovani's fault.

I won't let one thing ruin what we have going on between us. I've let enough people take from me over the last few years. There has to come a point when you say enough is enough.

Chapter 17

Giovani

After Harleigh left me standing in my own fucking bar, I left my parents to find their own way back to my house and took myself off to walk along the harbour. Everything is alive in the distance, over in Sunny Beach. It's party central in parts. It's at moments like this that I love being here in Old Nessebar. It gives me time to clear my head, think about the evening I had with Harleigh, then the atmosphere my father caused. I growl into the night sky. I've given my parents the benefit of the doubt when Lucca goes off on one, but maybe I've just never seen the vindictive side to my father. Maybe I didn't want to believe that man who raised us could be horrible to one of his own. Maybe my father has been good at having a go at Lucca without me noticing he was in the wrong.

I don't know what to think anymore. I just feel stupid. What on Earth will Harleigh think of me now? I've spent so much time getting her to relax around me, and now it could have all been for nothing. I wouldn't blame her if she never wanted to see me again.

My phone buzzes in my pocket and I take it out to see a message from my brother.

Lucca – Just heading home. Where are you?

Me – I'll be five minutes. I'm just taking a walk.

Lucca's fingers must be on the ball, because I'm just getting my message sent when his messages are coming back to me.

Lucca – Is everything okay? What happened tonight? Harls said nothing, but I'm not stupid.

Even after my father upset Harleigh, she still kept quiet and hid her own hurt to protect my family. That's the type of woman she is. She's kind and timid, but will do anything to protect the ones she cares about. She might have faced a ton of shit in the past, but I don't doubt she'll come back fighting stronger each day. I just wish other people could see the woman I see. I wish she would let people in to see it.

Me – I'll talk to you when I get home.

I put my phone back in my pocket and hope and pray that my parents have gone to the spare room they use when they visit. I can't be bothered getting into it with them tonight. I'm angry and upset at the way Harleigh was treated. I won't let that slide. My bed is going to be empty and cold tonight and I think that's making me even crankier, because already I'm getting used to Harleigh being with me. When I'm alone, I feel like a piece of me is missing, like my soul is halved.

I walk up my street and look up at my house. It's lit up like a castle. My castle. My sanctuary. It's one reason I bought the house and didn't just stay at the hotel, because I needed to separate home from work. It's where I can kick back and relax, but the thought of entering this house tonight is killing me. It feels like a warzone and not somewhere I want to be.

I walk into my house and lock the door. I throw down my keys and walk into the living room. It's a nightly ritual to make sure everything is locked up safe before calling it a night.

I hear my dad raising his voice. I see Lucca making a cup of coffee and my mum sitting on the couch keeping out of it. I roll my eyes and shake my head, because this is just typical when my dad and brother come face to face with one another in private. It's getting bloody boring. They can't spend five minutes together and everyone around them suffers from it.

I walk into my kitchen, pat Lucca's shoulder, and instead of getting a coffee, I pull out a bottle of beer and nearly drain it in one go. I need something stronger for this shit. My patience is wearing thin.

"Dad, can you just give it a rest, please? There's no wonder Lucca stays here instead of coming home to Italy if this is what he faces all the time. He's a grown man now. He can live his life anyway he likes." I sigh, exasperated. "He's not doing too badly, either."

Lucca was only home a few minutes before me and this is what I walk into. Family can be a right pain in the arse, especially when you have a father like ours that sits on a pedestal thinking he's the king of everyone. He forgets that we're not little boys anymore. We've got lives of our own, not exactly what he pictured for us, but we're happy.

"He's here, sponging off you, living in your house. He needs to find his own path."

Lucca scoffs beside me and shakes his head. Our father really knows nothing about our set-up here. Yes, this is my house, but Lucca pays his way.

"Maybe if you'd stop and give him a break, you'd see that he's doing just as well as I am. We've just bought a new bar in Sunny Beach *together*. A joint adventure. I haven't had to bail Lucca out since he was eighteen. Just stop, because you're going to push everyone away. What you said to Harleigh tonight was bang out of order. I don't usually answer you back, but enough is enough. For the first time in…" I throw my head back, steady my breathing, and try to remember the last time I was happy. "… a long fucking time, I'm happy. I'm enjoying life. Why can't you just be happy for us for once in your life? We'll never be you, so stop trying to make us that way."

"Giovani, I thought I raised you better than to back chat me."

"You did, Dad. But I'm tired. I'm tired of you two tearing strips from one another. Mum and I are stuck in between you two all the damn time. How do you think that makes us feel? I'm angry at you tonight. In fact, I'm fucking livid. So, I'm going to take this bottle to my room like a good little boy and bid you all a goodnight. Hopefully, tomorrow, I can salvage something with Harleigh and apologise for your behaviour."

My dad sniggers. "She's a woman. She'll see your status and come running back."

I bang my bottle down on the counter and Lucca jumps beside me.

"There you go again, Dad. Judging people, expecting all women to be the same. Harleigh has been through so much heartache in her life, I'm surprised she trusts anyone. I might not have known her long, but she's a strong, independent woman, who won't ask anyone for help or support. So, if you want to remain under my roof for this trip, you'll apologise the next time you see her, and you won't say another bad word about her, or to her, ever again."

I walk away from my kitchen and head straight to my bedroom. I bang the door and try to take in a few deep breaths to calm my racing heart. I feel bad that I've left Lucca to deal with my parents, but if I know my brother like I think I do, he'll disappear to his bedroom too. No good will come from me being in that kitchen with them all any longer tonight, because I feel as hot-headed as Lucca usually is. I'll end up saying something I might later regret.

I take my phone from my pocket and contemplate calling Harleigh. I need to know she's all right, but at the same time, I don't want to come across as being pushy.

Fuck it. I dial her number and let it ring a few times. I'm about to hang up when she answers.

"Hello," she says sweetly.

"Hi." I clear my throat. "I just needed to check that you're okay."

"I nearly missed your call. I just got out of the shower and heard my phone."

The thought of her naked wet body makes me rock hard. I can visualise her delicious curves and perfect skin. The thought of her sends my body wild, my heart racing, and my mind going to the gutter. I can't help it when I'm around her.

"Are you still there, Gio?"

It's then that I realise I've turned silent as I'm stuck in my own head.

"Yeah. I'm here. Are you okay?"

"I'm okay. You?"

"No," I say quickly and honestly. "I had an argument with my dad when I walked in on him and Lucca arguing. And I'm missing you like crazy. The thought of you naked and wet… well, it has me in a spin."

"Well, I can't do anything about Lucca and your dad, but maybe I can distract you."

"Oh, yeah? What do you have in mind?" I smile at her playfulness.

"We can talk."

"As much as I love talking to you, I think it will take a lot more to get me out of my head tonight." I throw back the rest of my beer and put the empty bottle on the bedside table.

"Well, it's a shame you're on your own and not here. I'm fairly sure we could distract one another."

"I'm sure we could." I smile.

I love this bit of confidence I hear from Harleigh tonight. My father hasn't killed the progress I've made so far, so that's a bonus, I guess.

I stand up quickly, walk out of my room—the rest of the house is now quiet—and I leave through the front door.

"Tell me what you're doing." I feel myself breathless from walking quickly. I just hope it isn't too noticeable to detect until I carry out my plan.

"I'm just about to make a coffee before I call it a night. What are you doing?"

"I'm living life, beautiful."

I rush into my hotel, pass through the quiet lobby, and instead of taking the lift, I run up the stairs two at a time. For once luck is on my side and I make it up the stairs in one piece.

"Really? What's your idea of living life?" she asks me.

I practically run down the corridor and knock on Harleigh's door. I hold the phone to my ear and hear her sigh. She isn't getting my reply, but she is getting a special surprise.

"Someone is at my door. I'll call you back."

She hangs up and I hear her door click. She opens it warily, but the moment her eyes land on me, she smiles warmly, and I see her body relax.

"Giovani, what are you doing here?"

"Living life." I smile cheekily and put my phone in my pocket.

I push through her door, lift her into my arms, and her legs wrap around my waist. Our mouths crash together, and our hands collide with each other, trying to find a release. I need to feel her wrapped around my heart and soul. She needs to consume every part of me.

Harleigh's tiny short pyjamas leave me wanting more. I can feel my dick weeping already. I lay her down on the couch and devour her mouth, running my hand under her shorts and finding her wet core. She needs me just as much as I need her. I didn't plan on barging in here the way I did, but the moment I saw her, something switched inside of me and I needed her more than she could ever realise. In fact, right now, I think I need her more than breathing.

"Gio…" Harleigh cries out, but it only fuels me more.

I pull off my shirt and remove my trousers in the blink of an eye. I climb over Harleigh's delicious body and settle between her legs. She's wearing too many clothes for my liking. Together, we manage to make quick work of the offending items until we're both naked. I lie over her, nudge at her entrance with my engorged dick, and stare into her eyes. I run my thumb down her face, feeling her relax into my touch.

"I needed to see you so badly, beautiful."

"I'm glad you did," she rasps out.

Without one more word, I push into her hot, welcoming centre and ride out the magnificent wave of pleasure that shoots through me from one thrust. The sparks are electrifying. I've never felt this connection to anyone before.

Our bodies move in sync, and sweat is coating our skin. The feelings we're making together, the power and strength radiating from us both when we're together is euphoric.

"I'm not going to last long, babe. Come with me."

I reach between us and circle her clit, making her buck underneath me, her legs tighten around my hips as we both crash into the abyss.

I lean my forehead in the crook of her neck and try to gain back some normalcy in my breathing. My heart is beating so wildly that I feel like I'm going to pass out.

"I...I..." Harleigh stutters and laughs at her own lack of ability to even speak.

"I feel the same way, I don't think my brain could comprehend how I feel right now." I roll off her and pull her into my side.

We lie together in each other's arms for the longest time. I think she might have fallen asleep when she reaches up to my cheek and caresses my neck.

"What happened tonight that brings you to my door at this time?"

I take in a deep breath and let it out slowly. I'm stalling for time, because I don't know how to tell her that my family is driving me crazy without sounding like a spoilt brat. Some people are crying out for families and would do anything to have one. Yet, right now, I'd do anything to give mine away.

"My family. I walked in on my dad and Lucca having an argument and I snapped. I just told a few home truths that should have been told a long time ago. I hate myself for answering back elders, but good God, it felt great."

"Feel better?" She looks up and gazes at me through the moonlit room.

I nod. "I do now. All thanks must go to you for that."

"I've learnt that, over time, sometimes we've got to get a lot off our chests before we can move forward. It isn't easy to let go of something, Gio."

I nod. I know what she means. "I'm really sorry about what my dad said to you tonight. He had no right to say that to you and it pissed me off to see that hurt in your eyes."

Harleigh leans up on her elbow and smiles warmly. "We both know I've picked the right brother, Gio. I adore Lucca, in a brotherly way. I still plan on going to lunch with him tomorrow, but if that will cause you or him any issues, I can take off for lunch on my own."

"Don't be silly. I won't have you avoiding my brother because of my father. Lucca needs someone like you in his life, too. I think our guardian angel sent you here. Not only for your own healing, but for mine and Lucca's too."

"Do you believe in fate?"

"I never used to, but this time, coincidences just don't seem like enough."

I tuck away a stray strand of hair that's fallen out of her messy bun, and she lies back down on my chest. I tighten my grip around her, and we snuggle down into the cushions. I'll have to thank my designer for these luxury couches, because I never thought I'd be sleeping on one.

"Sleep, babe. I've kept you up long enough."

And if I have my way, I'll be keeping her up late for her full holiday.

Chapter 18

Harleigh.

Sitting at the dressing table, tying my hair back off my face, I take in a deep breath. Giovani wants me to go to his house for breakfast with him, Lucca, and his parents. Lucca is making a feast and I can't say no. According to Gio, showing his father that I won't be scared away by him is the only way to get through to him. I don't see why I have to show him anything, but I'll do anything to keep Gio happy.

My phone rings on the bedside table. I jump up and notice it's the unknown caller again. I sigh and answer, because I'm hoping that maybe one of these times it's my brother calling from work and not just some strange caller.

"Hello?" The dead silence is starting to get on my nerves. "Eurgh!" I growl out my displeasure and end the call. I don't even give a second chance to reply.

"Something wrong?" asks Gio from the bathroom doorway.

"Another silent call. My phone only usually rings for work and my family, but none of them come up as caller unknown. It's annoying me."

"Understandable. I'm sure it's nothing."

I nod in agreement. It's just that anything unusual sets me on edge. I know nothing can happen to me here in Bulgaria, but my head takes a while to catch up to process my thoughts rationally.

"Are you ready?"

I nod and look down at my feet. Gio raises my chin to make me look him in the eye. It's something I'm getting used to whenever he's around.

"I don't like when you feel on edge or insecure. But let me tell you something." I look into Gio's eyes and hold his gaze. The only people I usually give eye contact to are my students, because I don't feel threatened around them. "You have nothing to feel insecure around me for. Lucca and I will never do anything to intentionally hurt you. I can promise you that."

"I know. I never thought I'd be able to be this person around another man again, but you've given me hope, Gio. I feel like I'm ten feet tall around you. I have this confidence I've never had before, even before my ex."

"And that's the way it should be. No man should ever knock a woman off her pedestal. He should raise her higher, treat her like a goddess, bow to her feet."

"Spoken like a true gentleman."

"I'm glad you think so. Now, I believe I need to feed m'lady."

"Feed me to the sharks more like." We both laugh at my remark. "Do I look okay?"

"You look beautiful. You always do. Let's get out of here."

And that's all the encouragement I need to follow Gio out of my hotel room, try to forget about the butterflies swirling around my stomach, and raise my head high.

***

We walk into Gio's house and I've never felt as nervous as I do right now. I can smell the wonderful aroma coming from the kitchen. We walk in and Lucca and Margo are busy cooking at the stove. Gio tightens his grip on my hand and I follow him like a little lost puppy.

"Good morning." Margo comes around the counter and rubs her hands down her apron. She quickly envelopes Gio in a warm hug and comes over to do the same to me. "It's wonderful to see you again, my dear."

"Grazie, Margo."

"Come on. Have a seat, love birds. I've been slaving over the stove all morning," Lucca breaks the moment and we all laugh. Margo picks up her towel and flicks Lucca's bare legs playfully.

"He hasn't burnt the bacon is what he's trying to tell you." Margo winks at me. "Go, have a seat outside. Your father is outside already. Lucca and I will bring out the food."

"Can I help?" I ask over the counter.

"No. Absolutely not. You're a guest. Go sit and take the weight off your feet."

Giovani pulls my hand softly and I smile from Margo to him. Before we reach the patio, Gio pulls me in to place a soft kiss on my lips. I feel the heat creep up my neck, but I quickly forget that when someone clears their throat.

Gio and I part slightly, but he doesn't remove his hand from mine. He keeps a tight grip of it and leads me to the table confidently.

"Good morning." Gio speaks first as he pulls out a chair for me.

"Morning. You must have been out early," says Alex.

Gio shrugs his shoulders. "I didn't sleep here."

Alex looks between Gio and me as if he's assessing us and lifts his orange juice to take a drink. I'm pretty sure he took a drink to stop himself from saying anything uncalled for.

"Harls, coffee for you, right?" asks Lucca as he places down a pot of coffee on the table.

"You know me too well. We haven't had a chance to grab a coffee this morning."

"I thought as much. Here you go." Lucca holds out a large mug of coffee and I take it like my life depends on it. Spending time with Gio is making me a little more laid back and easier going, but coffee is still a necessity. It's my lifeline to get through the day.

"So, what do you all have planned for today?" asks Alex.

I sip at my coffee, hoping it makes me invisible, and watch the interaction between father and sons.

"Lucca is taking Harleigh for lunch while I catch up on some paperwork. What do you and Mum have on the agenda?" Gio asks.

Gio pours his own coffee and sits back in his seat.

"We might go exploring for a while. Have some lunch and see what happens next. Maybe you'd like to show us this new bar of yours."

"Maybe. Yeah. That's some of the paperwork I've got to sign today. Lucca has signed his part. Once we get the keys, if you're still here, we can take you over to see it."

"I think your mother plans on being here for two weeks."

At the thought of Alex and Margo being here for two weeks, my heart misses a beat. I just hope I can see the true person behind Alex's mask, because he always shows a different person, and I don't know who he is.

"Okay then. You should be able to see the new bar before you leave."

At that moment, Lucca and Margo come out with plates of food and place them in the middle of the large table. Everything smells delicious; bacon, sausage, eggs, hash browns, mushrooms, and tomatoes... I'm in heaven.

"Tuck in, Harleigh, because my boys have an appetite bigger than a bear."

We all chuckle around the table and I think I see a ghost of a smile from Alex. The light chatter around the table is there, but I can feel the strain. Lucca sits opposite me and Gio, but he only speaks when spoken to. His shades are covering his eyes so I can't get a feel for what he's feeling, and it annoys me that he's hiding behind a barrier.

"So, Harleigh, you're an editor. Have you edited for anyone I might have read?" asks Margo.

"Oh, I edit mostly for independent authors, but I do occasionally, when I have time, edit for a small publishing company called Lonely Hearts Publishing. If you haven't already, you must check out Italian author, Laura Rossi. Her books are a fabulous mix of dark and romantic."

I beam at Margo. I could talk about books all day long. It's a lifelong passion of mine. I think I take that from my mum.

"It must be a rewarding job."

I chew the forkful of bacon I have in my mouth. "It is. Seeing people's work come to life is magnificent. It's like I'm a proud mother seeing them succeed."

"No intentions of writing for yourself one day?" asks Margo.

I shrug and take in a deep breath. "Who knows? It was always my intention to pen something to paper, but life got in the way. Now I have some time and independence, you never know what will happen. I'll never say never."

I feel Gio's hand rub circles on my upper thigh, giving me a little bit of strength and courage from his contact.

"You all have plans for today?" asks Margo.

I smile warmly at her, because she's trying her hardest to keep the chatter flowing easily. It's a question that was already asked before she came outside to eat.

"Lucca and Harleigh are going for lunch, and I have my half of the paperwork to take care of this afternoon. Dad said you plan on going exploring," says Gio.

Margo shrugs. "Maybe. We're on holiday and we both need some rest and relaxation."

And that's how our morning continues with Gio's parents. It feels nice to be around other people. The whole morning is stilted but flowed with some encouragement from us all. I think Lucca was the only one who didn't initiate conversation, but no one made an issue of it.

I think I proved I'm not scared of Gio's dad. He could throw anything at me, and he still wouldn't be as bad as the life I lived with Martin. He could give me the third degree, make me feel small, and not approve of what Gio and I have here, but I'm not letting him spoil my holiday. I don't have much time left and I plan on enjoying every moment.

Chapter 19

Harleigh

We're eating our lunch in a pub called The Funny Pub. It's a small bar in Sunny Beach that Lucca says is the best. We've done some shopping in the small shops and market stalls along the promenade, had a few refreshments, and now we're all walked out. I didn't realise how much I'd missed a friend to do basic things with.

Now it was time for a refreshment and some sustenance. As much as I wanted a burger, I decided to have the fajitas and they're amazing. They're lick your fingers clean amazing.

"How are you really, Harls? It's just us now. No need to sugar-coat things." Lucca takes a bite of his pizza and stares at me softly.

I shrug. "I'm okay. I'm enjoying my holiday," I look around us just as everything is getting busier.

"I meant with what happened last night."

I lift my cocktail to have something to do with my hands. "I don't blame your dad for being protective of you both. I have a dad and two brothers who are the same. I'll admit what he said hurt me, but I'm a big girl. I'll get over it."

Lucca shakes his head. "Just don't ever back down where my father is concerned. Stand up to him."

I nod. Gio told me the exact same thing earlier this morning.

"Is that what you've had to do?"

Lucca sits back in his seat and throws his arm over the back of the other chair. "I never used to. I used to take it, believe it or not. The teen years kicked in, I rebelled, and I found a life for myself. Now, we just butt heads at every turn. I'm what you call the black sheep of the family."

I reach over and squeeze his clenched fist. I hate that he feels that way. No one should be made to feel that way around family.

"I'm sorry you feel like that, Lucca. You and Gio seem to have a good relationship."

"We do. The best." Lucca sits forward and covers my hands with his. "What Giovani did last night, spoke up for you to our father, he has never done that before. He always tries to keep the peace. But when I heard him sneak out late last night... well, I was glad he did. It was a big fuck you to our dad."

"I don't want to hurt Gio, Lucca. I'm not sure I'll ever be ready to jump into a relationship again. What's that saying, 'once bitten, twice shy'? Well, I guess you can say I'm bloody petrified of being in that position again."

"The difference is that Gio will never hurt you, and if he ever did, I'd kill him for you."

We both laugh and the dark cloud that loomed over us is lifted and the sun is shining brightly.

"So, Gin-ology, huh?" Lucca takes another slice of pizza, changing the subject.

"He told you?" I can feel the heat creep up my cheeks, because I hate being put on the spot. "I didn't think anything about the name when I said it out loud."

"Stop being nervous, it's only me. And he did tell me. We both love it. I haven't told Gio that I love it yet, but I'll let him sweat it out a bit, wondering if I'm going to contest the name."

"You're mean."

Lucca shrugs and winks at me. "Gio would think there was something wrong if I wasn't a wind-up merchant."

We sit in silence for a few moments, eating the remainder of our meals. It's nice to have company other than my family. I might have been on the edge about coming on holiday myself, but it has opened a multitude of opportunities for me. Opportunities I'm looking forward to exploring more of over the coming weeks.

***

I've spent a couple of hours here at the pool while Lucca and Giovani work. Lucca didn't want to leave me alone after our lunch, but I made him go because I'm a big girl. I love spending time at the pool. It's one thing I do a lot of on holiday, but this time I've had so much keeping me entertained that the pool has been the last thing on my mind.

My phone rings in my bag and I reach under my lounger to retrieve it. I don't look at the caller ID and just answer it. The sun is so bright where I'm sitting. I sit up and put my hat back on.

"Hello."

Silence. Heavy breathing soon startles me, and I pull the phone from my ear and see caller unknown written on the screen again. This is the first time I've had anything other than silence. The heavy breathing rattles me.

"Who is this?" I ask rather abruptly.

I'm getting pissed off that this is happening on holiday. I'm supposed to be relaxing, but these calls are putting me on edge. I look around the pool, but all I see is elderly people sunbathing, people swimming in the pool, and kids playing on the grass. There is nothing out of the ordinary and the phone call goes dead.

I pull the phone away and look at it like it's going to eat me. I just want to know who the hell is calling me several times a day.

"Hey." I don't look up. I'm transfixed on the phone in my hand. "Harleigh?" Someone's hand lands on my shoulder and I jump, dropping my phone to the floor. "Shit. I didn't mean to make you jump."

The figure bends down in front of me. The fogginess clears from my head and I can see clearly.

"Gio..." I breathe out with relief.

My heart is racing, my throat is dry, and mouth feels like it has sandpaper in it.

"Hey. You okay? You look like you've seen a ghost."

I shake my head. "I'm okay." I straighten up.

"Babe, talk to me. Who was on the phone that's got you so worked up?"

Gio sits down on the ground and takes my hands in his, rubbing circles over the back of my hand.

"It was just the silly calls again, heavy breathing and nothing else. It just got my back up. I'm being silly."

"And you've no idea who it is?"

I shrug. "I have my suspicions, but I don't know how he would have gotten this number. Gavin changed my number after…"

I feel the hairs on the back of my arms and neck rise at the thought of Martin being the guilty party. He won't know where I am, will he?

"Honey, I don't think you have anything to worry about. You'll go home and find out it was someone you know trying to get a hold of you."

I nod, straighten my back, and tighten my grip on Gio's hands. "You're right. I'm just being silly."

"You're not silly. It's only natural to worry after what you've been through. You're being cautious."

"You're right. Enough about me. How was your afternoon?"

I quickly change the subject, because the longer I dwell on it, the longer it will consume me.

"Not as good as yours by the sounds of what Lucca told me."

"It's good to know a guy that likes shopping, afternoon cocktails, and junk food."

Gio laughs. "The Neanderthal in my brother hasn't put you off?" he winks at me.

"Absolutely not. He's good company."

"What do you think about getting out of here?" Gio asks me.

"What do you have in mind?"

Gio jumps to his feet, picks up my bag, and throws it over his shoulder. "Let me show you."

He takes my hand in his and I follow him like a little lost puppy. Only, my hand encased in his is the only thing I need to feel on top of the world and forget the last ten minutes at the pool.

We walk through his hotel, passing holiday makers until we're at the back of the hotel. He takes out his key, opens the private door, and we walk through. It's clear that this is a private residence, because it's decorated more homely. It's peaceful and calm.

"Where are we?"

"This is where I lived, before I bought my own house. I haven't been here in a while, but going to your room was too far away." He rounds on me quickly and lifts me into mid-air. We get tangled in my bag over Gio's shoulder and we both laugh.

"Damn bag. That looked a little less messy in my head."

"Why don't you show me."

Gio untangles us and throws down my bag with a clunk on the tiles and looks up at me. "I hope you don't have any breakables in there."

"Nothing that can't be replaced."

My answer clearly satisfies Gio, because he stalks towards me like I'm his prey. My whole body feels like electric is pulsing through my limbs.

He pushes the straps of my dress down my arms and the garment falls to a puddle on the ground. I'm standing in my strapless bikini, staring up into Gio's eyes. His thumb rubs against my lips softly before his lips find mine and devour my mouth. Our mouths are connected ferociously; probing, duelling, exploring. If I could die from a kiss, then this would be one of those kisses. It leaves me gasping, seeing stars.

Gio lifts me off my feet and walks backward with me in his arms. We crash into something, but it doesn't deter our movements. I rip at his shirt, trying to give me skin on skin contact with him. There's too much clothing between us.

Gio puts me down on a couch and crawls between my legs, pulling his shirt over his head easily. He kisses down my chest, hooking his fingers at either side of my pants and pulls them down my legs teasingly slowly. I'm ready to combust. I need him now.

He kisses back up the inside of my leg and lands on my core. His tongue circles my clit, sucking, pulling it between his teeth. My body is writhing below him. Holding onto his head, moving him to places I need, sends me spiralling into oblivion. He kisses back up my stomach, pulling down the cups of my bikini, nipping at my nipples. I'm trying to get my breathing under control, but all he's doing is sending me spiralling again. He wriggles out of his shorts and gives me no warning as he plunges deep inside of me, hitting my cervix with the tip of his dick. I feel so full, but in a good way. I've never had as many orgasms in my life, but Gio is only satisfied when I'm sated.

"This is going to be quick, honey."

I can't even answer him. I grip my legs around his waist and pull him in deeper with my crossed ankles. Thrust for thrust, kiss for kiss, we climb higher and higher until we explode together. I'm seeing more than stars as Gio empties inside of me.

Gio rolls off me and pulls me into his arms. My head rests on his chest comfortably. I can feel his beating heart underneath my ear. It makes me smile that I can do that to a man. A man I like. If I could bottle up that feeling I would. It's the biggest boost to my confidence.

"I'm never going to get enough of you, Harleigh. I honestly don't know what I'm going to do when you go home."

And just like that reality hits me like a bucket of cold water. I'm going home in about three weeks' time. What will happen then?

I take in a deep breath, let it out slowly, and decide to speak my mind. One thing I love about Giovani is that he never judges anything I say. He's supportive, and for me, that's the biggest plus side. I've never had a relationship where the man has listened to me, put me first, and encouraged me to be me.

"I'm growing fond of you, too, Giovani." I look up from his chest and see him watching me closely. "We've not got long left before I go home."

"Then what, beautiful?"

I shrug. Tears fill my eyes and I look away from Gio's intense stare.

"Hey..." Gio pushes me onto my back and hovers above me. "Don't cry. We'll figure out something. All I know is, I'm not ready to say goodbye to you. I don't think I ever will be."

"It's scary, because I never thought I'd find myself in this position again. To be here with you, to trust you, it has taken guts. But the confidence I've gained in myself is something else. I think I like the person you make me."

"I'm glad you've noticed a difference in yourself, baby. I've noticed the difference too, and I love the person I'm seeing. I loved the person I crashed into on your very first day too. I think our broken souls connected in a way I've never felt before."

"Crazy, huh?"

"It is, but I'm looking forward to the next three weeks we have together. We've got so much more to see and explore."

"It must be boring for you, because you've seen it all before."

He shakes his head. "I'm seeing it with fresh eyes, Harleigh. It's like I can see again for the first time in such a long time. I have no barriers up to protect me. You have my heart and soul in your hands."

"I better not squeeze too hard then." I smile.

"Squeeze as hard as you like, just don't break me."

"Never." I reach up and capture his mouth with mine.

And in just a few days, my world has turned on its axis, but for the first time in my life, it's for a good reason. This holiday and meeting Giovani seems like it's too good to be true. As exciting as it is, I'm constantly thinking that something is going to tear it all away from me.

Good things don't happen to me... ever.

Chapter 20

Giovani

Another glorious week has passed with Harleigh by my side. We've spent every spare minute together, enjoyed each other's company, and made love so many times I can't even count. I like it. No, I fucking love it. Having this connection with another person is euphoric. Even more so, because I had given up on love a long time ago. I believed I was destined to be businessman of the year for the rest of my life. I never expected to have a need to share my life with another woman.

Spending every moment with Harleigh has changed me. Having breakfast, lunch, and dinner together, waking up beside her, smelling her coconut shampoo. I can even tell you how many lines she has on her face, because I've studied her beautiful features when she was sleeping. I can hear the little whimpering noises she makes when she's in a deep sleep. Every detail is engraved into my memory. I will never forget one moment we spend together.

Today, I had to take care of paperwork and Harleigh went to the beach on her own to read and soak up some rays. I think I've tired her out lately - and not just with the sightseeing - not that either of us is complaining. The last ten days has showed us both that we can't go back to life as we once knew it. Things need to change forever. This relationship can't be over at the end of her holiday. I won't let it.

"Hi, sweetheart," says my mum, as she places a plate of sandwiches down in front of me. "Roast beef and English mustard. Still your favourite, right?"

"Hi. Thanks. Yes, still my all-time favourite. I never heard you come home."

I look back at my house, but my father isn't anywhere in sight. Usually, where one is, the other isn't far behind.

"I didn't want to disturb you. You looked so busy with work. Your father went for a nap, so I thought I'd make sure you're eating and keeping hydrated," she sits down beside me at the table. "Someone needs to take care of you boys. You work too hard."

I put down the pen and take a bite of my sandwich. I didn't realise how hungry I was until I smelt the delicious salad decorating my plate.

"I'm perfectly capable of looking after myself, Mum. But, thank you. You saved me a job." I smile at my mother warmly.

My mother has always been the perfect mother, cooking and cleaning for us, teaching us right from wrong, and shaping us into the men we are today. Even now I have my own life away from home, she still takes care of me when she comes to visit. In fact, she spends most of her time in my kitchen, trying to entice me back home to Italy with all her delicious Italian food and recipes. I must put on several pounds every time she visits.

"How are you, sweetie?" She reaches over and squeezes my arm.

I nod. "I'm good, Mum. I'm really good, in fact."

She smiles warmly at me and I see her sparkling blue eyes. "I think that's all down to that beautiful young woman."

"Your guess would be right." I beam.

"Young love. I'm so happy for you. You deserve this happiness. I never thought I'd see you with another woman again."

I've never said it out loud to Harleigh, but I do love her. I know I do. I just don't want to frighten her away with words too soon. I'd rather show her with my actions. I'll take this relationship as slowly as possible. It will kill me if she decides a long-distance relationship isn't going to work.

"You haven't told her you love her, have you?"

I lean my arms on the table and look out into my garden. "I haven't. She's going home in less than two weeks. She's been through so much, Mum."

"When I first met her, I could see the pain in her eyes. But, each day that has passed, I've seen it less and less. You're a good influence. Just like she's a good influence on you. You can't pass up that kind of friendship and love."

I know the change I've witnessed in Harleigh, but to hear someone else say it is different. I'm glad she trusts me enough to let her guard down around me, but I don't want to push too far too quickly. We've got our whole life ahead of us if we're willing to give it a go.

"I'm so happy to see a genuine smile on your face."

"I'm always happy, Mum."

My mum scoffs and squeezes my arm tighter. "You might think you can fool me the way you fooled everyone else, but I saw the hurt and pain you've been harvesting over the last few years. It was going to take someone extremely special to get through that tough wall you built around yourself."

I open my mouth to speak, but then close it again. I thought I had been a good actor, but clearly not.

"One day, when you have kids of your own, you'll know what I mean when I say we see everything. A mother or father sees every little change in their child, no matter what age they are. Just like I can see how happy and in love you are today. I'm surprised you're getting any work done knowing Harleigh is out there somewhere, on her own."

My mum isn't wrong. I'm trying to work, but all I have thought about is Harleigh. I've thought about calling her to make sure she's got plenty of sunscreen on, making sure she's keeping hydrated. But, most of all, I'm imagining her wrapped in my arms. The thought alone has got my dick stirring to life in my pants.

"I've never felt this way before."

"My papa always used to tell me that when you find *the one*, every piece of your heart is complete. Your soul is as bright as a star. And when that happens, you're the strongest you can be. I can see that strength when you and Harleigh are together. I'm just sad you've both had to have heartache before you found one another."

"Things happen for a reason, right?" I take the last bite of my sandwich and sit back in my seat.

"They sure do. When I met your dad, things were different. We didn't have the time to court. We were married within six weeks of knowing each other. Now, you can build a relationship, watch and feel it grow, and nurture it to be strong and unbreakable. If you and Harleigh are meant to be together, you'll figure it all out. You'll find a way to make it work."

"I hope you're right, Mum."

My mum stands up, leans across to me, and places a kiss on my forehead. "I'm always right, sweetheart."

And with those parting words, she walks into the house, leaving me staring at her retreating back. I can always rely on my mum to tell it to me straight. She has always been a strong, independent woman that I look up to. She taught me to treat women right, to respect them. *'Never treat a woman the way you wouldn't like being treated yourself.'*

Without my mum, I don't know where I'd be because my father is the complete opposite of her. He always provided for us financially, but he lacked parenting skills. Maybe that's why he and Lucca butt heads at every turn. They lack a connection. Lucca and I are more like our mother. We feel things. We're not your typical Italian males that provide for their family and leave the rest up to the woman. When, or if, I have kids, I want to be a hands-on father. Maybe I can thank my father for teaching me what not to do.

I gather up all my paperwork, make a neat pile, and get up to file it away for the day. I've done everything I set out to do. Now I'm ready to take some time for me.

I'm actually enjoying taking me time, and I never thought I'd hear myself say that.

Chapter 21

Harleigh

I've sat on the beach for about two hours, maybe even longer. Time just rolls away from me on days like today where I'm stuck in my own head. I've enjoyed this quiet time, just to gather up some thoughts and try to make sense of them. Not that it has worked, because my thoughts and feelings are still confusing the life out of me. My head and heart are not on the same page. My past is still colliding with my future, making it difficult to move on.

I give up trying to analyse everything now, because I'm just making myself sink further into a dark hole. A place I hate myself for sinking to, because I've spent too much of my life there already. I take out my book and get transported to another world by the marvellous Toya Richardson. Her new beach read series is the perfect escape from reality. But, reading this type of story lets me see that holiday romance can exist, not only in books, but real life too. The end of my holiday doesn't need to mean the end of Giovani and me. Our holiday fling can be so much more if we want it to be. We just need to be open with one another and willing to work at a relationship. I need to stop being timid and just voice my thoughts and feelings.

Eurgh! Of course I want everything with Gio, but who says he wants the same? He'll probably be glad to see the back of me at the end of this. I'm surprised I haven't scared him away with the amount of baggage I come with. I'm damaged goods; that will never change. With the amount of physical and emotional scars I have, I'll always feel broken. I heard Martin's derogatory comments often enough to know that I'm useless, worthless, and no man will ever want his sloppy seconds.

"What did I ever see in you?"

Martin grips my hair tightly and pulls my head backwards. It feels like he's about to snap my neck and there isn't one thing I can do to stop him.

"You make me sick. The day you walked into my life, everything changed." He spits in my face.

"You can let me go," I cry out. "I'll leave."

He laughs hysterically. He looks like a maniac. A mad man possessed.

"I'll never let you go. You're mine. To do with as I please. You'll be seen and not heard from this moment on, do I make myself clear?"

"Yes." I sob.

He pushes me away from him and I land on the floor on my backside. I look up carefully in time to see him walking out of the kitchen. I take a huge breath in and out, feeling my lungs fill up with pure air. This is what happened because I answered the phone to his boss. Well, I didn't know it was his boss. The phone rang and it was only me here. I take it I'm not to answer the phone at all now. Just another rule in my forever growing list. I'd be as well stuck in a cage. Animals have more freedom.

My phone rings and snaps me out of my depressive state. I'm having one of those days when my rational self can't remain positive. It's too easy to think about the negative things and let them tear me down. The least little thing transports me back to the past. I'm not strong enough to walk around with a permanent mask on that says I'm okay all the time. Occasionally, it slips, and the whole world gets a glimpse at the dark place I'm in. While I've been here in Bulgaria, that dark abyss hasn't consumed me as much as it did back home. I've been happy. I've felt alive for the first time in God knows how long. I feel free here.

"Hello." I sigh.

"Hey. What's wrong?" asks Gavin.

I turn onto my back on the lounger and take in a deep breath. "Nothing. I'm at the beach."

"Yeah, and I know you better than that, doll. Every time I've spoken to you lately you've had a burst of energy. Today, you sound..." He pauses for a few moments and I move the umbrella to block out the sun from my face. "I don't know. You sound defeated. Talk to me."

"I'm just being silly."

"Let me be the judge of that. Now, start talking before I book a flight out to Bulgaria."

I sit up quickly because I know my brother is impulsive where I'm concerned. It won't take him two seconds to book a flight and be on his way out here.

"I'm just having one of those days where I let my dark thoughts consume me. I'll be fine."

"And...?"

I bang my hand down on my knee, because my brother is like a dog with a bone when he wants to know something. He won't let go until he gets what he wants.

"I just…" I look out to the sea and try to think about what to say. "You know this guy I've kind of been seeing a lot of?"

"Uh-huh."

"Well, I really like him, Gav. He's kind, considerate, attentive, and he treats me like a queen." I take in a deep breath. "I've never felt so cherished before."

"Okay. So, what's the problem?"

"It will have to end when I come home." I sigh dramatically.

I feel like a child being told I'm not allowed something. I want to stand in the middle of this beach and have a tantrum. I know how childish that sounds, but that's the mood I'm in today. Why couldn't Giovani and I cross paths when he lived in Scotland? Why now, when we're a million miles apart? Okay, that's probably a slight exaggeration, but it feels like we live different lives. His life and my life are so extremely far apart.

"Harls, why does it need to end?"

"Because I live in Scotland and Giovani lives here for part of the year and goes travelling for the other part. He's easy going. Whereas I'm this hermit that likes routine and structure." Tears sting my eyes, but I'm determined not to let them fall.

"Listen to me, because I don't want you to do something irrational. Think about your life, Harleigh. Think about where you've come from, what you've faced, and then think about the last couple of weeks. If you like this Giovani guy, tell him. You can work anywhere in the world, doll. Whether you teach or edit, you can do it freelance. By the sounds of it, this guy has made his mark on you and I know you wouldn't just let anyone roll into your life. That means he's special. That means you have something worth fighting to keep."

"I don't know, Gavin. What if he doesn't want to be a permanent thing? What if I've just been another notch on his bedpost? He's got everything going for him. What do I have to bring to a relationship?"

"First of all, I don't know that guy, but he doesn't seem like the type to use you and leave you from everything you've been telling me. Secondly, you're the most amazing woman I know. You might not be a business person or a millionaire, but you're a bright, hard-working woman, and any man will be lucky to have you. That bastard you got away from is just a prick and you need to stop letting him control your life. I hope I never have to see him again because I will kill him with my bare hands."

I cringe. I know he would cause damage to Martin, and as much as I don't care about him, I do care about my brother, and a criminal record would hurt his career.

"He isn't worth it, Gavin. I got away. I'm free. I've been happy here. I've found a little piece of myself. I just wish I could erase these negative thoughts forever. It's like it doesn't matter how much positivity I show, there is always a bucket of negative energy just waiting to land on my shoulders."

"In time, I think you will learn that good things are meant to happen to you. You'll realise that you deserve every drop of happiness and love that comes your way. I can't tell you how proud I am of you. You went on this vacation, embraced the change, and grabbed every opportunity you could. You sound like you've found a lot of yourself in Bulgaria."

"I have, and that's what scares me. I don't think I'll ever feel like this back home, and I should be comfortable where I call home."

"Just enjoy the rest of your holiday. Think about yourself, your future, and what you want to happen next. Only you can make these decisions. Speak to Giovani. You never know, you might be going through the exact same turmoil, just afraid to broach the subject with one another."

"You're right."

"I always am right, sis. Now, what are you doing?"

"I'm on the beach with my book. Gio had some work to do today, and I wanted to get some sun, sea, and sand. I thought the tranquil setting would be good for me."

"Spoken like a true sun worshipper."

"You know me too well. How's everyone back home?"

"All good here. I break up for two weeks' holiday next week. Looking forward to some R&R."

"Good. You work too hard."

"You sound like Mum."

"That's not a bad compliment. Mum gives out good advice."

"I beg to differ on that one. Anyway, remember what I said. I'll call you in a couple of days, but call me if you need me to be your sounding board."

"Thanks, Gav. I love you."

"Love you too."

I hang up the call because my tear-filled eyes spill over. I was glad I kept it together while I was talking to Gavin, because I couldn't deal with his overprotective arse flying out here. I know he wasn't joking.

Could I really give up my life back home? Could I really live out here and travel with Giovani? Could I go home and forget all about Gio and what we've achieved over the last couple of weeks?

So many questions and time is of the essence.

That call has just made me more confused, because I have a lot of questions I need to work through in my head before I bombard Giovani with them. I need to be sure of my decisions, because once I voice them, there is no going back.

Chapter 22

Harleigh

I take the last forkful of my omelette I ordered for lunch and sigh with contentment. I found a small café in the middle of Old Nessebar. It reminds me of a French café I once visited in Paris when I was eighteen. I'm glad I was lured in with the blue and white checked tablecloths and china cups I saw people sitting with outside. I came inside because I think I've had a bit too much sun today. My head is bursting, but I'm not sure if it's the sun or my constant over-thinking things. I've tried to avoid Giovani as much as possible the last two days, but I can't avoid him forever. He's only going to burst into my room to find out what on Earth is going on. I've sent him texts to tell him I'm okay and I'm just exploring, but I know it was pitiful. It was a poor attempt to get him off my back.

I'm doing what I do best – hiding. I'm hiding from my problems instead of facing them head on. I'm afraid of everything, but I think disappointment is my biggest fear of all. I don't want to believe that Gio will just walk away from us next week, but the reality of it happening is high, and I wouldn't blame him one bit.

"Can I get you anything else, Miss?" the waitress asks as she lifts my plate.

"No, I'm stuffed. Thank you. Can I have the bill, please?"

The waitress nods in a friendly manner and walks away quickly. She hasn't had a minute since I arrived here today. She must be hot and bothered, but she has never once showed it. She returns with my bill inside a leather pouch and puts it down beside me. I leave my money with a tip and make my way out. The moment I exit the café, the heat hits me. I didn't think it was that cool inside, but it clearly was when I feel this stifling heat.

I've been out since eight this morning. I did a bit of shopping, had breakfast and lunch out, and now I'm going to make my way back to the hotel to spend some time in the cold pool. I know I won't be able to hide out there, but maybe Gio has given up looking for me.

The moment I enter the hotel, I see Gio and Lucca at the desk, having a heated conversation with a middle-aged gentleman. I smile weakly and attempt to carry on walking, but within moments, I feel Gio's hand on my back, guiding me out back and into a room labelled *office*. He bangs the door closed and I jump as he walks up behind me and rests his hands on my hips. I can feel the warmth from his hands, but a shiver runs through me. I'm not sure if it's fear or anticipation of what's about to happen.

This conversation was inevitable when he caught up to me.

"I'm not sure whether to hold you tight or yell at you for leaving me hanging the last couple of days." He kisses my neck. "So, are you going to tell me what's going through that pretty little head of yours?"

"Nothing," I breathe out as he kisses up my neck to my ear. "I just needed some space to get my head on straight."

"And would you care to enlighten me to allow me to get *my* head on straight?"

I turn in his arms, because the more he touches or kisses me, the more my brain isn't engaging in what I'm meant to say.

"I was just going to head to the pool to cool off."

"Come to my house. We can use the pool there, and you can start talking."

"You looked kind of busy out there." I point over his shoulder.

"It's taken care of already. It was just a pissed of guest that caused a little ruckus for Jerald when he was cleaning the gardens. Besides, I've had plenty of time to work the last couple of days you've been avoiding me."

"I haven't…"

Gio holds his finger over my lips and halts my words. "Don't insult me by saying you weren't avoiding me. I think we both know you were, but now I'd like to know why so I can fix it."

"Are your parents not at your house?"

He shakes his head. "They're at Bourgas for the day, shopping. Their taxi won't be picking them up until five." Gio looks down at his watch. "We have a good five hours before they arrive home."

I take in a deep breath and let it out slowly. "Okay. Lead the way."

I'm not sure what will come of today, but it's clear that I'm hurting Giovani and myself more by avoiding certain topics. I need to pull up my big girl panties and stop acting like a child.

KM Lowe
TIDAL LOVE

Chapter 23

Giovani

Holding Harleigh's hand as we navigate through the street to get to my house is a feeling that I've missed so damn much. I know she's pulled away the last couple of days and it has killed me. I've been impossible to live and work with. I've snapped at everyone, including my parents and Lucca. Everyone is keeping their distance from me and I hate it. I hate every thought and emotion I've felt over the last couple of days. And now, I'm about to find out what was the cause of it.

We walk into my garden and up into the house. Harleigh kicks off her sandals and I can see the relief in her face.

"Have you been walking a lot?"

She nods. "I went shopping earlier and had some lunch in a little café. The heat is killing my poor feet."

She walks across the cold tiles behind me and I open the patio doors. Harleigh walks over to the pool and sits down on the edge, letting her feet dangle in the cold water. I kick off my shoes, pull my t-shirt over my head, and dive into the pool. I'm hoping by doing this, it lets Harleigh see that I'm no threat and she can say whatever she has to say.

"You are such a Neanderthal." She giggles and wipes the splash of water off her face.

My body instantly jolts alive, not at the cold water, but at the sound of her laughing.

"So, walking and eating out is how you've managed to avoid me. Has it been worth getting sore feet for?" I swim over to her, grab her foot in the palms of my hands, and massage them firmly. The sound of her moaning at my touch is the biggest turn on I've ever had.

"That feels so good."

"Good. Now, if you want me to continue this, you need to start talking. I'm not psychic. I can't read your mind, beautiful. I can only make this right if you tell me what's going on. What made you avoid me?"

I take in a deep breath.

"I got scared. I thought that maybe a goodbye would be easier if we didn't see much of each other for the remainder of my holiday."

I nod. "And has it? Has it made anything easier? I just had to touch you in my office and you were like putty in my hands. I know you feel this connection, Harleigh. Why run away from it?"

She shrugs and tears roll down her cheek. I let go of her foot and pull her into the water with me. She gasps as the cold water consumes her. I hate to see her in any pain, especially if it's down to me.

She wraps her arms around me and buries her face into my neck. Her legs wrap around my waist and I just hold her until she's ready to continue.

"I don't want us to end, Gio." She sniffles and pulls back enough for me to feel her warm breath on my face.

"Good. Because neither do I. In fact, I'm ready, if you want me to, to give everything up and move back to Scotland, if it means we could make a go of it. I'll do anything, Harleigh. I want this. I want you. We can work it out, but you need to talk to me."

"I don't want you to give anything up. I'm just not sure how we can make this work as a long-distance relationship. We've been miserable apart, and it's only been two days."

"Come and live here with me. Spend the rest of the season with me and see what you think. If you don't like it, we can re-evaluate then."

"Are you asking me that because you want me to be here, or are you asking me that because you think it's what I want to hear?"

Giovani pushes me back against the pool wall and runs his hands through my hair, capturing my cheeks between his hands.

"I'm asking you this because this, what we thought was maybe a holiday fling, has turned into something serious. I don't think I can live without you in my life, Harleigh. I've made everyone's life a living hell the last couple of days. I'm surprised I have a family or staff left. Tell me what you want."

"I need to go home next week, Gio. I have my house to sort out and my work to consult. But I think I might like to have a shot at this whole relationship thing. I'm not sure how good I'll be at it, but if you'll have me, I'd like to come back out as soon as possible. Gosh, what am I saying?" She shakes her head and smiles. Her eyes are twinkling, her smile reaches her eyes, and her skin is glowing. She's always beautiful, but at this moment, she looks like a sweet angel.

My angel.

"I hope what you're saying is that you're ready to live a life with me."

"I am. I really am."

"Scared?" I ask her.

She shrugs. "I think I'd be lying if I told you I wasn't, but most of me is excited and thrilled about this fresh start. I'll never be scared of you, Giovani."

"Good. You've made me the happiest man alive. I've been going out of my mind with worry the last couple of days. I wanted to use the hotel's key card and burst into your room last night, but Lucca told me to get a grip or he'd take all the keys away from me."

We both laugh at that. The sound of laughter is like music to my ears.

"I'm pretty sure you'd have got away with breaking and entering since you're the owner and all."

"Yeah. My actions sounded a lot better when my head was a scrambled mess. Now, with you in my arms, I can see how wrong and unethical that would have been."

"Good. I'm sorry I ran. I will try to stop hiding my feelings and talk to you more. Hiding solves nothing. I know that. Sometimes I just get stuck in my head."

"And we'll both work at this relationship every single day. I have my flaws as well. I snore and leave the toilet seat up."

Harleigh laughs. "I'm sure I can live with that if you can live with me and my baggage."

"What baggage? The way I see it is, that baggage you're talking about has shaped you into this wonderful woman I'm holding in my arms."

"I'm glad you think so. Now, I don't want to push my luck, because I don't deserve you, but that foot massage was amazing. That foot isn't even sore now."

"You want the other one done?" I ask cheekily. "What's in it for me?"

"Me coming to live with you isn't enough?"

"When you put it like that…" I pull back from her and lift her foot up into my hands. I'll massage every part of her body before this day ends.

I know we'll have a lot of ups and downs along the way, especially as we settle into a routine. But the difference here is, we both want this. Anything is possible if you both want something so badly.

Chapter 24

One Week Later

Harleigh

I've been dreading this day for the last two weeks. Today is the day that I've got to fly home to Scotland, break the news to my family that I'm uprooting my life to live spontaneously, and hand in my notice to my work. I've got so many people to let down and that breaks my heart, but the thought of never seeing Giovani again sends me to a place I'd rather not be. Thinking about the life we could have together feels right. The only thing that feels wrong is flying home to Scotland, living a life full of fear and uncertainty, and never returning to Bulgaria. Nope, for once in my life, I'm doing something for me.

I sit down on my suitcase, because Gio is just going to take it to his house for me. It seems pointless taking it home to come back with so much more. At least I can fly back with some important things I'd like here with me. The rest can go into storage until I'm ready to settle down somewhere permanently.

"All ready?" Gio leans in the door frame and folds his arms over his muscular chest.

"As ready as I'll ever be." I stand up and walk over to Gio, lean my head against his chest, and he runs his hands up and down my arms. "I've got my hand luggage ready for the plane. I'm all good. Did your parents get off okay?"

Margo and Alex were supposed to go home last week, but they extended their trip so they could see the new bar being refurbished. Instead, they flew out at eight o'clock this morning.

"Lucca took them to the airport on time. He said they got off okay. I would have liked to be a fly on the wall during that trip to Bourgas. I'm pretty sure Lucca would have thrown them through the airport doors and left."

I laugh. "Yeah, me too. They've been getting on a little better lately."

"Hmm, until the next time."

"Or maybe your dad can see that Lucca is making something of his life here."

"Maybe. Anyway, is someone picking you up in Glasgow when you land?"

I nod. "My mum, dad, and brother are picking me up. I bet Gavin has told them everything I've said and done since I arrived here. I'll be put through a Spanish inquisition."

Gio tightens his arms around me and backs us out of the room. Usually, he's backing us into a room, ripping my clothes off, and worshipping every part of me. It's a stark contrast, and I'd much rather the latter option, but we need to leave in about twenty minutes if I'm going to be on time.

"They've missed you, beautiful. And, if you want to Skype me in on the chat you have about coming back out here, I don't mind. I'd like to put their mind at ease that I'm not going to hurt you."

"They'll be eager to meet you. I don't know why I'm nervous. I'm an adult. I know my family will be happy for me once they've got the interrogation out of the way. It's just..." I sigh.

"It's just that you don't like the unknown."

I look carefully at Giovani. In such a short space of time, he has got me worked out.

"You've probably hit the bullseye with that remark."

"Come on. My brother wants to see you before you head off. I did tell him it wasn't like he wasn't going to see you again, but you know what he's like."

"I'm glad, because I want to say goodbye to him. Well, not goodbye, just a see you later. I've become extremely fond of you both in such a short space of time."

"Good, because it looks like you're stuck with us both now."

"That's no hardship, honey." I lean up on my toes and seal my lips with Gio's. It's soft and passionate, nothing that would suggest we need to get moving soon if I'm going to make my flight on time.

We pull apart at the same time and Gio leans over to pick up my hand luggage and suitcase. I'm pretty sure I could help him, but he's a stubborn male who likes to show off his strong side, and I love that about him.

"We'll give the luggage to Lucca in the bar and he'll take it to the house for you, saves us having to leave now to hand it in. It gives you an extra ten minutes downstairs with him."

I nod. I "You look so put together. Yet, here I am, flapping like a bird."

"Looks can be deceiving, beautiful. Inside, my heart is breaking at the thought of you in Scotland without me. But it's only for a short time, right?"

"Absolutely. Wild horses couldn't keep me away from here and you guys."

We leave the hotel room and I take one last look around before the door closes and I hear the click of the lock. Every step away from the room fills me with dread. I know I'm being silly and overreacting, I just can't help it.

We take the elevator down to the lobby; it's quite busy with guests arriving and leaving. Today is going to be a busy day for the staff.

We enter the bar and Lucca spots us straight away. He walks over to us and throws his arms around me, lifting me off the ground and spinning me around in circles. "I'm going to miss you, Harls."

"Me too." Tears sting my eyes.

I'm only saying goodbye to Lucca. What the hell am I going to be like saying goodbye to Gio at the airport?

"You'll be back soon though, right?"

"Yeah, as soon as possible. You'd better stay out of trouble for me coming back."

"I can't make any promises." Lucca winks at me.

"This is Harleigh's luggage that needs to go over to our house. Just put it in my room and I'll take care of it when I come home." Gio hands over my luggage and just leaves himself with my hand luggage. I could get used to traveling light. I hate baggage areas at the airport.

"Got it. Have a safe trip, Harls. Call, text, Skype, whatever. Just keep in touch."

"I will."

Lucca leans in and places a kiss on my cheek. And in the blink of an eye, he's walking away with my luggage in each hand. I'm glad he used his initiative and realised I was struggling with the goodbyes.

Giovani wraps his arm around my shoulders and I lean my head onto his shoulder. We walk out of the hotel and Gio's car is waiting for me. This is it. This is the last time I'm going to see this place for a while.

"You'll be back before you know it, beautiful."

"Yeah," I say sombrely.

I'll be back.

Chapter 25

Harleigh

I've just landed in Glasgow, and since I've just got hand luggage, I can exit straight through arrivals. But, before I meet my family, I turn on my phone and type out a text to Giovani.

Me – I've landed safely. I'll give you a call later when I get home. Missing you already.

I've no sooner hit send and I'm getting a reply. It instantly puts a smile on my face, but I feel the effects of being so far away from Gio and Lucca. Lucca has become a good friend to me too. He's the first person outside of my family and Giovani that I've confided in, opened up to, and enjoyed his friendship.

Giovani – I'm missing you like crazy too. Today has been very dull without you. I hope your night with your family goes well. I look forward to speaking with you later. Love Gio.

It's five p.m. here, and already I feel exhausted from the jet lag. Or, it's from all the crying I've done. I spent the first two hours away from Giovani in tears, sobbing my heart out and feeling sorry for myself. I kept my sunglasses on for most of my flight. I probably looked ridiculous, but it would have been better than seeing me with tears and snot dripping down my face. If anyone noticed me crying, they turned a blind eye and allowed me to wallow on my own.

The moment I exit through the arrivals door, my parents and Gavin are standing with big smiles on their face. The smiles don't last long when they see me close up. They've seen enough of me upset and in tears, they'll know the signs.

Gavin walks towards me slowly and envelopes me in his arms. The moment I feel that he's got my weight, I break into tears. I can't hide my emotions any longer.

"I've got you, sissy. I've got you."

I don't know how long we stand in the middle of the arrivals lounge for, but the next thing I feel is my mum and dad hugging Gavin and me tightly.

"Is this all your luggage?" asks my mum.

I manage a nod of my head through my gut-wrenching sobs.

"Let's get out of here, guys," says my dad.

Gavin puts me down on the ground and holds his arm around my shoulder. We leave Glasgow airport and everything is in a blur.

"We've got a table booked at The Bruce. Seb's going to meet us there after his work," my mum tells me.

I don't think I'm ready to sit and eat dinner, but I owe it to my family to tell them everything. I don't like hiding things from them. I've held enough back from them because of Martin, and when I got away from him, I promised myself and them that I would always be open and honest with them.

***

We sit down at our booth for dinner, and Gavin sits beside me, and takes my hand in his.

"What can I get you all to drink?" asks the waitress.

"I'll just have an orange and lemonade, please."

"No cocktails?" asks Gav cheekily.

I shake my head. "No. Honestly, I've drunk my weight in cocktails during my holiday. My liver needs a break," I joke.

"So, sweetheart, you had a good trip?" My mum breaks the awkward tension around the table.

"I did. It was the best."

"You don't seem thrilled to be home, sweetheart."

My dad reaches over and squeezes my arm.

I nod and Gavin squeezes my hand tighter. I think he knows what's coming and he's silently telling me that he's got my back.

"I've got a lot to tell you all. And…" I trail off as the waitress places our drinks down.

Right now, I'm wishing I decided to have an alcoholic drink for Dutch courage.

"What's on your mind, Harls?" asks Gav, pushing me to continue.

"I…" I take in a deep breath and hold my head up high. If the last four weeks have taught me anything, it's that I should always face life head on, and not looking down at my hands or feet.

"Sweetheart, you can tell us anything," my mum says.

"I met someone in Bulgaria. I met two people. Giovani and Lucca. They're brothers. They lived in Glasgow their whole life, parents from Italy, and now they run the hotel I stayed in. I met them on my first day in Bulgaria, and I've spent pretty much my whole holiday in their company."

"Aww, that's good. I'm glad you met people and had fun. You'll have to invite them over the next time they're home."

"I'm not staying," I blurt out.

I wanted to be tactful about this conversation, but I just need to get it over with.

"What do you mean, you're not staying?" my mum probes.

"I'm moving to Bulgaria, Mum. It has broken my heart leaving Giovani behind today. He was ready to give up everything to come back here, for me, but this doesn't feel like home for me anymore. It hasn't for a long time. I don't want to hurt you, because you've all done so much for me, but while I was in Bulgaria, I found out a lot about myself. I'm confident. I felt alive and free. I wasn't constantly looking over my shoulder. I liked myself for the first time in..." I blow out a breath.

"Did you know about this?" my mum asks Gavin.

He shakes his head. "I knew there were going to be some changes, but I didn't know to what extent. But I have to say, I'm so proud of you, Harls. Speaking to you the last couple of weeks has been like speaking to a new person. And, for what it's worth, I like Giovani."

"You haven't met him." I laugh.

"No, I haven't. But I have stalked him on social media. And if he makes you happy then that's all that matters to me."

"Thank you." I swipe away at the stray tears falling down my cheeks.

My mum and dad are staring at me like I've grown horns. I just want them to talk to me, ask questions, scream at me... anything, is better than silence.

"Mum? Dad?" I push for them to say something.

"Are you happy, sweetheart?" asks my dad.

I nod. "I've never been happier."

"And you have everything you need to make this transition work?"

"I need to resign from work, pack up my house, and book flights back to Bulgaria, but I have everything planned."

My dad nods, but my mum is still just staring at me.

"Mum."

"I don't know what to say. I'm a little lost for words."

We stare each other down and everything is carrying on around us. Gavin clears his throat and sits forward.

"Mum, what would you rather, she stays here and falls into a black hole with no room for return? Because, let's face it, we were all worried before this holiday. Look at this..."

Gavin takes out his phone, goes to my Facebook timeline, and shows my mum and dad some of my pictures with Giovani. Just looking at the pictures again stabs my heart.

"What do you see, Mum?"

Tears fall down my mum's cheeks and she tries to swipe them away before causing a scene. "You look happy, sweetheart."

"I am, Mum. I wouldn't be doing this if I wasn't happy. I wouldn't be doing any of this if there was a tiny part of me that wasn't sure. I want to do this. I want to live life, see places, and be with someone I..." I clear my throat. "Someone I love."

And that's the first time I've said that out loud, but I like it.

"I'd like to meet Giovani before I give you my blessing."

"I'd like you to meet him. In fact, he's agreed to do a Skype with you guys. I'll come by tomorrow and we'll do it. It will give us all tonight to digest everything. I'm not doing this to hurt any of you. I love you all."

"We know, sweetheart," My dad reaches over the table and takes my hand. "We love you so much. It's a lot to take in, but if you're happy then I'm happy."

"Thank you, Dad."

"And I'll just have to come back to Bulgaria with you to meet Giovani and Lucca." Gavin nudges my side and I laugh.

I knew this would be happening at some point, because although he's stalked Giovani, it won't count until he's seen him face to face.

"I wouldn't expect any less from you, bro."

"Good. Now that's settled, let's order, because I'm starved," says Gavin dramatically.

And that's how our family reunion started. It went better than I anticipated, and for that, I'm happy. I just need to get my mum on side and show her that I'm doing the right thing.

***

"Are you sure you don't mind dropping Harleigh off at home?" asks Dad.

"No, I don't mind," said Gav. "It will give us time to catch up."

"Okay, sweetheart. We'll see you tomorrow. I'm sorry Sebastian got caught up at work, but we'll fill him in tonight, and he'll be there tomorrow for this Skype call." My mum leans into me, places a kiss on my cheek, and squeezes me tightly.

"It's okay. I'll see you tomorrow."

I part from my parents and walk over to Gavin's car that he left here earlier today, because he travelled to the airport with Mum and Dad.

"That wasn't too bad, huh?"

I shake my head and climb into his car. "It went better than I thought. I just hope Mum comes around."

"She will. She just needs some time to digest it all. You're her little girl and that will never change."

I nod and totally understand why she's acting the way she is. Gavin pulls out of the car park and heads out onto the main road. It will take us about twenty minutes to get to my house, and I'm looking forward to taking off my shoes and having a nice hot bath.

"You have a glowing tan."

"Yeah, the weather out there is unbelievable."

"I know I've said this a lot lately, Harls, but I'm so proud of you."

"You have said that an awful lot, but it means a lot. I have you to thank for my change of luck."

"Nope. This is all on you, sis. I just gave you a…" Gavin pauses and looks in his rear-view mirror. "Some arsehole is trying to run into the back of us."

"What?" Our car moves quicker, and I look behind us.

"This car is trying to run us off the road."

The car behind bangs into us, shunting us forward. I scream and hold onto the door tightly. Our car is all over the road, trying to get out of the way safely.

"What's going on?" I cry. "Who would do this."

Bang.

My heart is pounding in my chest. My nerves are shot. Will this ever stop?

The road we're on is long and winding. There is no way for us to get off. We speed up and try to get away from the car but it comes up alongside us, and it's now that I get a glimpse of who's behind the wheel – *Martin*.

Fuck! This is all we need.

"He's lost his ever-loving mind," shouts my brother as he tries to keep our car on the road. "Move over, dick!"

"Gavin, he's going to kill us!" I scream as he rams into us again. This goes on for about two miles, until a lorry comes along on the other side of the road.

"Gavin!" I scream, but it's useless. There is nowhere for us to go. Another ram in our side and our car gets turned over and we roll for what feels like forever.

I hear the smashing of glass, crunching of metal, and the smell of rubber burning. Everything is a blur. My head is banging and I can't move. I feel paralysed. I want to scream and try to get to my brother, but nothing happens. I can't speak. I can't even cry.

Oh my God, Giovani.

Giovani is my last thought before everything goes black.

Chapter 26

Giovani

I've heard nothing from Harleigh since earlier today. I'm worried about her. Her phone is either dead or she's got it switched off. I've sent her lots of texts and voicemails. I've even sent her Facebook messages, but there is nothing from her. I'm going out of my mind with worry. I just wish she would let me know she's okay. I have no idea what happened with her family when she arrived in Glasgow. Did they make her change her mind? Is she afraid to tell me?

I bang down my phone on my desk and pour myself another whiskey. Yeah, I've hit the hard stuff. I need a distraction and only alcohol will do the trick.

Lucca walks into my office and sits down at his desk.

"Have you heard from Harleigh?"

"Nope!" I snap. "You?"

Lucca shakes his head and throws a pen at me. "Of course I've not. I would have said if I had. She's probably got carried away reuniting with her folks and lost track of time."

"Yeah."

As rational as that sounds I can't help but think there is something wrong. I have this gut feeling that's usually spot on.

"I have no way of contacting her family. We didn't exchange numbers or addresses."

"Can't you contact her brother via Facebook? He commented on one of her pictures of you both. They both did, I'm sure."

"Yeah, that's a plan. If I don't hear from her in the next couple of hours, I'll do just that. I don't want to look like a stalker."

"I'll take this." Lucca reaches over my desk and drags the bottle of alcohol away from me.

I want to scream at him for taking what's mine, but I know he's right. I shouldn't be under the influence when I hear from Harleigh. I need a clear head.

"Go have a lie down. I'll wake you if I hear anything."

"Maybe." I stand from my desk, grab my phone and wallet, and leave my office. I walk through my hotel and go straight to Harleigh's room. I've told everyone to keep the room empty just now. It's the only room that still smells of her perfume. It's the one room where I still feel a connection to the woman who has stolen my heart and soul.

I climb onto the bed, hold her pillow tightly, and close my eyes. I've been awake since 4.30 this morning, since my parents were flying back to Italy. I feel like the walking dead, and the whiskey has just made that worse.

***

"Giovani!" I hear being yelled somewhere in the distance.

Am I dreaming?

"Giovani, wake up." I feel myself being pulled several different ways.

I wake up with a jolt and sit forward. I feel disorientated. Where am I? I look around and see that I'm in a hotel room. Harleigh's hotel room. That's all the recognition I need to snap my attention to Lucca.

"What is it? Where's the fire?"

"It's Harleigh."

"What?" Dread fills my stomach. "What's wrong with her?"

"We got a call here at the hotel from her father. I took it because I wasn't waking you up until I knew what was going on. Harleigh and her brother have been in an accident. She's in Forth Valley Royal hospital. I don't know the details, but it doesn't sound good, Giovani."

My whole body feels like it's in shock. I can't seem to think about what I need to do or say.

"What do you want to do?" asks Lucca.

Lucca sits beside me on the bed and squeezes my shoulder.

"I thought she was just ignoring me," I breathe out.

"Never mind that now. Harleigh needs you, Gio."

I nod. I need to get to her. I need to see her with my own two eyes.

"I need a flight. I need to pack a few things and go to her."

"I'll book a flight. I'll book you a rental. Just go home, pack a few things, and I'll call you with all the details. I'll print everything you need and meet you in the office."

"What about you?"

"We both can't go. Someone needs to hold the fort here. Just keep me updated on everything."

I climb off the bed like I'm in a drunken state. My legs feel like jelly. My head is a jumbled mess. I wish I'd kept her here with me. I wish I told her to forget about going home. Better still, I should have gone home with her and faced her family. Now, I'm flying across the globe to see Harleigh, to see what state she's in, and meet her family.

Harleigh has been through so much. She deserves a fucking break. What happens if I never get to see her beautiful eyes again? Her sweet voice. Her infectious laugh. I'll crucify anyone who has hurt her. They might have taken away the one and only thing I've loved in such a long time.

Chapter 27

Harleigh

Beep. Beep. Beep. I've listened to this continuous beeping for what feels like hours. Only I can't do anything to move or turn it off. I don't know where I am or what I'm doing. I feel someone holding my hand, but I can't see who. The uncertainty of everything is making me anxious. The beeping gets quicker and rings in my ears.

"Doctor."

Mum. I can hear my mum, but why can't I see her?

"Please, it has been fifteen hours. What news do you have?"

Where the hell am I? Why is she talking to a doctor?

"I'm afraid it's still too early to tell, Mrs Harrison. Your daughter has received a head trauma. We need to see if the brain swelling reduces on its own with the medication we've administered."

"And how long will that take?"

"Every patient reacts to brain trauma differently. We can't put a time on it."

"But she will wake up, right?" asks my mum.

"It's too early to tell. I'm sorry I don't have any better news. Maybe you should go home and get some rest."

"No. I'm not leaving my baby girl. Can you tell us anything about my son?"

"He's doing well. Your husband is with him. He has a broken arm, a broken knee that we've splinted, and a few cracked ribs that were causing his breathing issues when he arrived. But we've got on top of the pain and he's already asking about his sister."

"Good. Some good news is better than none. Just promise me that you'll keep my babies alive," my mum cries.

"I promise, I'll do everything I can."

And everything goes silent again. I try to think about what's happening, but nothing is making any sense. I can remember leaving Bulgaria and coming home, going for dinner, and leaving... Oh my god, Martin. He tried to run us off the road. I'm alive. Gavin's alive. Giovani will think I'm not returning to Bulgaria if he doesn't hear from me. He'll be going out of his mind with worry. Why can't my life be straightforward? Whenever something good happens, a bucket load of shit follows.

I need to get myself fit and well to return to Giovani. I must return to Giovani.

Chapter 28

Giovani

It feels like days ago since I heard that Harleigh was hurt, but it's exactly twenty-four hours. I had to wait until the next morning before I could fly out to Scotland. Once I got on my flight, I think I counted down the minutes until I could see my girl again. I just want to hug her, hold her, and tell her that everything will be okay.

Everything has run smoothly. It's just after lunchtime and I pull into the hospital car park. I haven't heard anything from Lucca or Harleigh's family. I'm not even sure if they know I'm coming here, but I couldn't stay away. I just need to be with her.

I jog into the hospital, read the sign, and follow it until I reach Ward 23. When I come to the ward doors, I see the ICU sign.

Holy fuck! Please be okay, baby.

I ring the buzzer and wait for someone to answer.

"Hello, how can I help you?"

"Hi, my name is Giovani Russi. I'm here to see my girlfriend, Harleigh Harrison."

"Hold on, please."

The line goes quiet for what feels like an eternity. What is taking them so long? Why can't they just push the button and let me in?

The door in front of me opens and two guys come out. One is older than the other, but I can tell that the younger one is some relation to Harleigh, because they have the same eye and hair colour, and the same face shape.

"Giovani." The older man holds out his hand to me, and I shake it.

"Hi, how is she?"

He shakes his head. "I'm Rodger, Harleigh's dad, and this is Sebastian, her brother."

I hold my hand out to Sebastian and he shakes it. "I've heard a lot about you."

"All good I hope." He smiles weakly.

"Absolutely. Now, can someone please tell me what's going on? I'm imagining all sorts."

Rodger nods. "After dinner yesterday, Gavin was driving Harleigh home. They were run off the road by Harleigh's ex. I don't know what she's told you about him..."

I cut Rodger off. "I know about Harleigh's past."

He smiles at me. "Good. That saves me some explaining as to how we got here."

"Please, tell me that the bastard is dead?" I ask.

I don't care how crazy that makes me sound. I detest this guy already and I've never met him.

"You'll get on with my sons because they have the same attitude where this dick is concerned, but to answer your question, no he's not. He escaped with minor cuts and bruises. I believe he's in police custody as we speak. The truck turned over trying to get out of the way, which, from what we believe, is what caused Gavin's car to crash and roll down the embankment."

"And Harleigh and Gavin? They're okay, right?"

"Gavin has a few broken bones. He's here because, when he arrived, he had trouble breathing, but so far so good. He's desperate to be by his sister's bedside. Harleigh is another story. She's on a ventilator at the moment to help aid her recovery. She has a lot of swelling on the brain from the impact of the accident, but we need to be hopeful that she'll pull through."

I take in a deep breath. "But she will pull through, right?"

"No one can answer that until she wakes up, son."

I feel the bile rise up my throat and I try to keep it at bay. I feel sick to my stomach that Harleigh was just so happy a few days ago, and now she's lying here fighting for her life. How is that fair?

"I know she'll be happy to wake up and see you here, though."

I nod. "I hope you don't mind. I had to come and see her the minute my brother told me. He wanted to be here too, but one of us had to say behind."

"Of course we don't mind. Come on, I'll show you where she is. Her mum is with her now."

"I don't want to intrude."

"You're not. Come on."

I'm not sure if I'm thinking about Harleigh's family, or if I'm just chickening out now I'm here. I'll fight the biggest businessmen, but put someone I care about in a bad way and I'm a chicken-hearted bugger with my heart on my sleeve.

We walk through the white, sterile corridors. It's so quiet and peaceful. I've never been in any ICU department before, so it feels alien to me.

"She's just in here." Rodger points to the door he's pushing through.

Sebastian pats my shoulder and carries on walking down the corridor. I take it he's going to his brother's bedside. I pause at the open door. I can see Harleigh's bed at the end of the curtain. I walk into the room and see Harleigh's mum first. She smiles warmly at me, even though she doesn't know who I am.

Rodger pulls the curtain back enough for me to see Harleigh lying hooked up to all sorts of machines. Her beautiful face looks battered and bruised. Her eyes are black and blue and swollen, she looks like she's done ten rounds with a heavyweight champion.

Tears roll down my cheek. I can't hide my emotions. I don't care how weak that makes me look.

"Giovani, this is Margery, Harleigh's mum. Marge, this is Giovani."

She stands up and comes over to shake my hand. I can see where Harleigh gets her looks from; the resemblance is uncanny.

"It's nice to meet you, Giovani. I've heard a lot about you from Harleigh."

"Yeah…" I breathe out the breath I didn't realise I had been holding. "I'm sorry. I didn't know things were so bad. I thought I was going to walk in here and hold her, tell her that everything would be okay. Now…" I choke back my tears.

"Well, you can come and talk to her. The nurse said she may be able to hear us. It might help her recovery if she hears voices she recognises."

Margery takes my hand and leads me over to the seat she just got out of. She makes me sit down and places my hand over Harleigh's. I feel her warm skin, and it reminds me of many happy times we held hands in Bulgaria.

"I'll just be next door visiting Gavin. I didn't want to leave her alone, but I believe she's in good hands now."

"Thank you. I'll take care of her."

"Anyone that hops on a plane from Bulgaria to be by my daughter's bedside gets my approval," says Margery as she picks up her handbag. "Welcome to the family, Giovani."

I don't know what to say to that, so I just rub circles on Harleigh's hand until the room is empty. I want to scream and shout. I've never felt this angry and fearful in my life. I can't lose her… not now.

"You've got this, baby. You're a strong woman. We have the rest of our lives to lead when you're ready."

And I will wait for her for as long as it takes.

Chapter 29

2 weeks later

Harleigh

Beep. Beep. Beep.

I don't know how much longer I can hear that persistent beeping. It's driving me crazy. I can hear my family around me daily, but I can't open my eyes. Nothing I do is allowing me to open my eyes and return to my life. I've heard my mum cry and shout at everyone. I've heard Giovani pleading with me to wake up and come back to him. They might be a mess, but my heart is broken that I'm causing them so much hurt and pain.

"Good morning," says a voice I don't recognise.

"Good morning, doctor. Any news?" asks my mum.

"Last night's CT scan showed a significant improvement. Harleigh's vital signs are improving daily, even off the ventilator. Things are looking positive. We've just got to wait for her to regain consciousness."

"You've been telling us this for two weeks, Doc," says Gavin.

"I'm sorry. I did tell you that people with head trauma react differently. I've seen someone with a worse head condition wake up in a couple of days."

Nope. No more. I need to wake up. I squeeze my hand tightly, hoping that the hand I'm holding feels it. *Please, someone feel it.*

"Holy shit. Sorry. She's squeezing my hand," says Gio.

I'm happy to know its Giovani's hand in mine. It has been there for so long that I don't want to let it go.

"Harleigh, can you open your eyes, beautiful?"

I feel Giovani's hand rub across my head and down my cheek. I'm feeling more power over my body than I have in so long.

I groan. I can hear it. I can feel how dry my throat and mouth are. It's probably as dry as the Sahara Desert. I try to move my lips to speak, but they're dry and stuck together.

"Come on, Harls. It's time to wake up now, sissy."

Gavin.

I feel my eyes pop open and everything in front of me is white and blurry. It takes me a few moments to make out shapes and figures, then I see Giovani hovering over me. He's the only person I can see other than the doctor.

"Hi, beautiful."

"H-Hi." I croakily blurt out.

I'm not sure if that's the dry mouth, or if it's because I've never spoken for a while, or if there's something wrong with my speech. Either way, I don't care. I'm awake.

"Welcome back, Harleigh. How are you feeling?" asks the doctor.

I attempt to shrug my shoulders, but I'm not sure if I got it right. It probably looked very messy.

"I-I'm O-okay."

"Why is she stuttering, doc?" asks Gavin.

"Your sister has suffered an extremely big head trauma. She may need a lot of rehabilitation before she returns to herself, and it's possible that there may still be some weakness from the accident."

"We'll do all we can to help, beautiful. I promise." Giovani leans in and places a tender kiss on my cheek. I feel my body smiling at his contact. It's the best thing I've felt since I was in Bulgaria.

"I-I'm sorry." Tears roll down my cheeks, but Giovani rubs them away.

"You have nothing to be sorry about. We just need to get you better now, and then we can look to the future, just like we planned."

"I-I I-like that idea."

I feel like I've lost so much time being stuck in this hospital. I don't know what has happened with my family, the dick who put me here, or with Giovani and Lucca. I know for sure when I'm ready for it, I will make the most of life. I will live each day like it's the last. Love hard, cherish everything, and make memories that are worth making. Hopefully, in time, I'll be able to make so many good memories that it will erase some of the bad.

Epilogue

One year Later

Harleigh

Twelve long months have passed since my accident. I don't know why I say accident, because it was intentional. Martin had set out to hurt me. In fact, we all – investigators as well – think that he set out to kill me. It later came out that all the silent phone calls I had in Bulgaria were from him. He had been following my family around for weeks to try and find out where I was. When he saw me coming out of the airport, he set his plan into action. I hate to remember that day because it holds a lot of upset for me. Not just the accident, but also leaving Giovani behind. That could have been the last time I saw him. I'm lucky to be alive. I must believe my guardian angel was watching over me that day.

"Harls, are you all ready?" asks Gavin as he enters my bedroom at my mother's house.

"I am."

My brothers and Giovani have been packing up everything for me over the last twelve months. Giovani and Lucca spent the winter here with me instead of traveling like they usually do. It was good to get to know them away from their work.

Giovani and Lucca have taken things back to Bulgaria with them to save me doing any lifting. Giovani has been back here for three days, and today is the day I'm getting ready to fly out to Bulgaria to start my new life. It has been a long time coming, and I'm more than ready.

We're all flying out this afternoon, and on Saturday, Giovani and I are getting married in the hotel. The moment I got out of hospital to start my rehabilitation, Giovani got down on one knee and proposed. Of course, I accepted. I couldn't not agree to marry him.

"You don't look ready." Gavin picks up my final suitcase with my wedding dress inside.

"Of course I am. I've been waiting for so long for this day."

"Have I told you lately that I'm so proud of you?" I nod. "What you've done to get here, learning to speak properly again, walking without a frame. You're amazing."

At the memory of everything I've had to overcome to get here, to get the all clear to fly, has been nothing short of a miracle. I could have lived with a stutter or stammer, but I was determined not to let that accident take anything from me. Now, I still have a slight limp from the broken leg that didn't heal properly. It needed to be re-broken and pinned once I was alert and complaining of pain. It was a long recovery, but it's all in the past. I'm alive. It could have been a lot worse.

"I couldn't have done any of this without you all."

"You've got a good guy down there, Harls. I'm happy for you both."

"Thank you. I'm glad you all get along. It makes my life so much easier." I giggle.

"He knows if he ever hurts you, I'll have his head on a stick."

"And we all know he's never going to hurt me."

"I know. Just don't spoil all of my fun, Harls. Come on, let's get out of here. I'm dying for some R&R."

"Me too. It's hard to believe it's been a year since I was last there."

I might have had a terrible year, but my life starts today. Martin is locked up in a psychiatric ward. I hope he stays there for a long time. I won't let him take any more from me. Not now, and not ever.

Epilogue

Giovani

"Come on, bro. You must have memorised those vows by now. You've been staring at them for the past two hours." Lucca pulls the paper from my hands.

"I don't want to screw this up. I know it's only family and a few of our friends from here, but it means a lot to me that Harleigh knows how much I love her." I sigh.

"And if she doesn't know that by now, she never will. Come on. We need to make our way to the conference suite."

I nod, stand up, and leave my office. Harleigh will be here in the next ten minutes, and I don't want to be late.

I walk through the hotel and the wedding balloons are dotted around the lobby. Harleigh doesn't want to close off the bar today, she just wants everyone to have fun. I can't argue with her. I'd hang the moon and stars for her if I could. Today is all about her, the love we share, and two families coming together as one.

We walk into the conference suite that we've only ever used once for a wedding reception. It's all set out beautifully. My staff and Lucca have done us proud in my absence.

"Wedding planning might be your speciality, bro," I tease.

"Yeah, not likely to happen again." Lucca punches my arm.

I look around the room eagerly. My mum and dad are talking to Harleigh's mum. Everyone has been getting on well since we came together three days ago. For two families that have never met before, you wouldn't be able to tell. Even my dad and Lucca have been on their best behaviour, and I hope that's one bridge that lasts.

The soft harp music starts to play through the speakers. It's soft and delicate; exactly how I see Harleigh.

Everyone starts to take their seats and Lucca and I are standing up front waiting for Harleigh to make her appearance. I would have been quite happy to marry Harleigh in Scotland, but she was adamant that wasn't happening until she could come back to Bulgaria and we could marry where it all began for us. I could see her point. Scotland holds so many dark memories for her, but here, it's a happy place.

Lucca nudges me in the ribs and points to the back of the room. Harleigh is there holding onto her dad's arm. She's dressed in a smart white strapless dress. She looks like an elegant princess with her hair all pinned up. She looks like an angel.

My angel.

I take in a few deep breaths to steady my racing heart. Rodger walks Harleigh to me and passes me her hand. I accept it without a second thought. I can't wait to be Mr and Mrs Russi. I never thought I'd say that, but Harleigh changed everything for me. She made me want the two point four kids and a white picket fence.

"Are you ready for this, beautiful?"

She turns and winks at me. "I've never been more ready, Gio. You and me together is the only thing that makes sense. I can't wait to live this life with you. I love you."

"I love you too, beautiful."

And if this is only the beginning, I can't wait to see what life has in store for us, because I can guarantee that we'll still be living this lifestyle when we're grey and old.

Our holiday romance has turned into a tidal romance, mixed with many emotions, but now our love will only ever blossom and grow as we move forward. Nothing will ever pull us apart again.

If anyone was interested in the authors I mentioned in this book, check out the following information below.

Italian Author, Laura Rossi. Laura writes a mixture of contemporary, sports romance, and dark romance. There is something for everyone, but my favourite is Skins. It's Amazing!

Laura Rossi –
https://www.goodreads.com/author/show/2381552.Laura_Rossi?from_search=true&from_srp=true

My best friend and fellow author, Toya Richardson. The beach reads series mentioned in this book are exactly what they suggest – a perfect holiday romance that you can devour on the beach like Harleigh. You'll be transported to some amazing destinations around the world.

Toya Richardson –
https://www.goodreads.com/book/show/39907155-destination-love

A Look At KM Lowe's Books

Paranormal Books

The Beautiful Life Trilogy

The Smile (Book 1)

The Smile – New Beginnings (Book 2)

The Smile – Forever After (Book 3)

The Guardian Shifters

Lisa – Coming Of Age (Book 1)

Jasper – United Together (Book 2)

Kevin – Always and Forever (Book 3)

Joel – Alive And Kicking (Book 4)

Jasper – Taking Control (Book 4.5)

Callum – Past And Present (Book 5)

Julian – A Clean Break (Book 6)

Contemporary Books

It Was Meant To Be

A Country Escape

What Becomes Of A Broken Heart – A Coffee break read (A short novella)

A Different Christmas

Home for Christmas

Celebrations (A collection of celebratory short stories)

Burning Hearts Duet

Burning Hearts – A Dark Loss (Book 0.5)

Burning Hearts (Book 1)

Romantic Suspense Books

Burning Love (A Burning Hearts Novel)

Shawland Security:Book 1

Shawland Security:Book 2 (Coming Winter 2020)

Coming Soon

Shawland Security: Book 2

Clay Shawland has always been the 'Joker of the pack'. He's the one everyone goes to for a fun time. However, just lately, fun is the last thing on his mind. In fact, he doesn't even know what that word means anymore.

When Clay left the army, he got his life back on track. He had a new business, friends, and everything going for him…except the only woman he has ever loved…Shay.

Shay was abducted by the enemy - while out on a mission with her squad - and is now stuck in the middle of a human trafficking ring. Her only concern is getting out of there to return to her family…and Clay. But as each day passes, that determination dies a little more. Stuck inside the medical wing inside the enemy's camp, help is too far away, but that doesn't stop Shay from digging around for answers. Secrets are uncovered leaving her and her loved ones vulnerable.

Clay and his brothers are determined to find Shay dead or alive. They need closure, and they'll stop at nothing to get it, even if that means they lose everything they've worked so hard for.

Once again, Shawland Security needs to up their game to save their loved one.

Goodreads -

https://www.goodreads.com/book/show/45710369-shawland-security

MULTI-GENRE AUTHOR

KMLOWE86@OUTLOOK.COM

 /AUTHORKMLOWE   /AUTHOR_K_M_LOWE

 /KMLOWE86   /KMLOWE

Facebook – www.facebook.com/authorkmlowe

Twitter - www.twitter.com/KMLOWE86

Instagram - www.instagram.com/author_k.m_lowe

Goodreads - www.goodreads.com/KMLOWE

Bookbub – https://www.bookbub.com/authors/km-lowe

Youtube –
https://www.youtube.com/channel/UC3OPT6GR821cMeGDJN_-nng

Readers Group –
https://www.facebook.com/groups/1493820667568743/

The Guardians Readers Group -
https://www.facebook.com/groups/399414513862608/?ref=bookmarks

Printed in Poland
by Amazon Fulfillment
Poland Sp. z o.o., Wrocław